AMERICAN ATHENAEUM
A MUSEUM OF WORDS

THINGS THEY CARRY
SUMMERTIME 2013

A Sword & Saga Press Publication

MASTHEAD

Editor-In-Chief
⇒ Hunter Liguore

Poetry Editor
⇒ John Dudek

Fiction and Non-Fiction Editors
⇒ Jan Nerenberg
⇒ Heidi C. Parton

Cover Photo
⇒ "We'll Be Waiting," Mika Matson-Ray by Jessica DeHaan

American Athenaeum is a cultural magazine that features fiction, poetry, essays, opinion, author book reviews, and other literary contributions. Each journal explores the world of words like a patron explores a museum—by offering a view of the past, right up until the present. We consider this journal to be a museum of artistic endeavors, filled with cultural appreciation and stories that not only teach, but demonstrate the frailty of the human condition.

About Us: One of the very first literary journals was published in London, 1798, by August Wilhelm and Karl Wilhelm Friedrich Schlegel. It was called *Athenaeum*. Keeping with the vision of the first journal in offering a kaleidoscope of voices, *American Athenaeum* strives to publish a diverse web of voices that represents "the people." Whether writers know it or not, they are influenced by the world around them. Each shares a slightly different worldview and experience. And just as we can look back into the past and know and understand and learn through the voices, it is our hope that through this publication each of our smaller worlds will grow a little bigger.

Published by Sword & Saga Press, Copyright, 2013
www.swordandsagapress.com
Warriors Wanted

WELCOME

Editorial
⇒ THINGS THEY CARRY by Jan Nerenberg

America Talks
⇒ THE WEIGHT OF BEARING WITNESS by erica l. kaufman

Poetry
⇒ HAPPY BIRTHDAY by Lynn Hoffman
⇒ ROAST CORN MAN by Robert Truscott
⇒ GHOST AND ILLEGALS by Lee Passarella
⇒ LIFELINES by Shirley Kuo
⇒ RD. TRIP GODS by Victoria Boynton
⇒ SOKUSHINBUTSU by Duke Trott
⇒ SITALA: SHE WHO MAKES COOL by Berwyn Moore
⇒ THE COST OF WAR by Major Chris Heatherly

Views From the Past
⇒ THE BURNING OF OUR HOUSE by Anne Bradstreet (1612–72)
⇒ INVICTUS by William Ernest Henley (1849–1903)
⇒ TEWA SONG OF THE SKY LOOM by Anonymous
⇒ VIETNAMESE FOLK POEM by Anonymous
⇒ THE NEW COLOSSUS by Emma Lazarus (1849–87)
⇒ THE FIRST TELEPHONE CALL by Alexander Grahame Bell (1847–1922)
⇒ THE CYCLONE by Frank L. Baum (1856–1919)
⇒ WHAT TO A SLAVE, IS THE FOURTH OF JULY? by Frederick Douglass (1817–95)
⇒ MEDITATIONS by Marcus Aurelius (121–80 CE)
⇒ WHAT IS AN AMERICAN? by Hector St. John de Crevecoeur (1735–1813)
⇒ SUMMER DAYS AT MOUNT SHASTA by John Muir (1838–1914)

Essays
⇒ LANGUAGE LESSONS by Catherine Jagoe
⇒ TWO ANCESTORS AND TWO ANSWERS by Jeff Rasley
⇒ BLACK DOLLS by Amanda Wray
⇒ LETTING GO OF HISTORY by Cristina S. Mendez
⇒ RAGS IS RICHES by Charles Tarlton

Compassion City
⇒ CLOSE TO MY HEART by Gail Jeidy

Fiction
⇒ I WASN'T THERE by John Poblocki
⇒ AND I'LL BLOW YOUR HOUSE DOWN by Susan Levi Wallach
⇒ ROOTS OF GREEN by Rachel Routier
⇒ A HISTORY OF ART by Jennifer Falkner
⇒ RECOVERED MEMORIES by John Mueter

Voice of Endangered Species
⇒ MOON SWALLOWS by Stosch Sabo

1 Bookshelf
⇒ THE BOOKS-I-OWN-BUT-HAVEN'T-READ-BOOKSHELF by Mardra Sikora
⇒ A READER'S MEMOIR by Sydney Avey

Interview
⇒ THE ROLLRIGHT WITCH: AN INTERVIEW WITH ARTIST DAVID GOSLING by Jan Nerenberg

Artistic Views of the World
⇒ CONSTITUTION AVENUE by Brett Busang
⇒ SKULLS WITH RED STRIPES by Ira Joel Haber
⇒ BANANALAND by Christopher Woods
⇒ HEAD FLOATING ON GROUND by Ivan de Monbrison
⇒ SUN HAT by Amelia Jane Nierenberg
⇒ THE MUSE by Cassie M. Seinuk
⇒ JACK KEROUAC by Loren Kantor
⇒ HONEY DO by Patricia Merlino

Author Book Reviews
⇒ LEAVE OF ABSENCE by Tanya Peterson
⇒ BIRTHING MY NOVEL by Holly Lorincz

Wisdomgrams

Homographs
⇒ HOMOGRAPHIES by Richard Kostelanetz

Serialization
⇒ THE STORY OF DR. DOOLITTLE (Ch. 4) by Hugh Lofting

A SNAPSHOT OF OUR UNIQUE DEPARTMENTS

⇒ *AMERICA TALKS*
Your voice being heard in the world

⇒ *POETRY*

⇒ *VIEWS FROM THE PAST*
When we look at the past, we are called to remember, to see where we've been, and consider, where we will go tomorrow.

⇒ *ESSAYS*

⇒ *FICTION*

⇒ *VOICE OF ENDANGERED SPECIES*
Writers adopt species at risk of extinction

⇒ *COMPASSION CITY*
What is your view of the future? We imagine cities of compassion.

⇒ *INTERVIEW*

⇒ *1 BOOKSHELF*
What memories does your bookshelf hold?

⇒ *AUTHOR BOOK REVIEWS*
Authors share their work in their own words

⇒ *WISDOMGRAMS* *Everyone has a little snick of wisdom. (To submit your own visit our website.)*

⇒ *SERIALIZATION*
Join us each month as we read the latest chapter of a longer work.

Things They Carry 6

⇒ *EDITORIAL*

THINGS WE CARRY
by Jan Nerenberg

We all carry things: books, backpacks, pictures, perhaps, a good-luck token of a family memento... and we all carry memories. It has been said that we become the sum total of all we have read and experienced in our lives, from being presented a sun-soaked dandelion delivered by a grubby, dimpled, little fist, to feeling the rifle's retort on a soldier's shoulder, the fallen etched permanently in the retinas of his or her eyes.

We carry firsts with us like a personal talisman: first date, first kiss, first love, first child. We sorrow over our first goodbyes, be it through death, romantic break-ups, or seeing a loved one leave for parts unknown, sometimes fraught with danger, not knowing if they will be seen or held again in mortality.

With this issue we share our love of country, both the good and the bad, standing with hand over heart when our flag passes in a parade to show our respect for those who volunteer to serve in far-flung places. Those that serve carry with them our love, gratitude and prayers. From a history, rich with those who served in uniforms of all colors, to those who offer services that make the world a better place within our neighborhoods, we salute you. For it is those who carry on doing the best they can each day—the soldiers, farmers, doctors, dentists, writers, dreamers, scientists, mothers, wives, husbands, brothers, and children—both born and those only hoped for—who carry on in the background, creating a home to return to.

This month's cover, "We'll Be Waiting," hits not only a personal level for me, but also a visceral one. It still impacts me, as much now, as it did the first time I saw it, although fear no longer rises at the thought of the father, so far away from home and in harm's way, carrying the love of wife, family, and country, along with a uniform, rations, and armament.

The cover photo, taken by Jessica DeHaan, features a pregnant Mika Ray, who is married to Corporal Trever Ray, who served in the 31st MEU in the Asia/Pacific. Eden Leigh Ray was born on October 5, 2011. In Mrs. Ray's own words:

"I was thirty-nine weeks pregnant, with our first child, when this picture was taken. My husband had been deployed when I was just fourteen weeks pregnant. He got to meet our daughter when she was just shy of two months old. Being the wife of a Marine means making sacrifices. Today I'm blessed to have my family of three together!"

Home safe at last. But there are many who have yet to return home. Our prayers continue for all those who now stand in like situations, for the mothers and fathers who say goodbye; the brothers, sisters, and children who are proud, but don't quite understand the separation; the sweethearts, who face profound loneliness; as well as the priceless unborn who await entrance into an uncertain future.

In considering the things we carry, I'm reminded of a poem I read in my youth by Robert Frost:

> Two roads diverged in a yellow wood,
> And sorry I couldn't travel both
> And the traveler, long I stood
> And looked down one as far as I could
> To where it bent in the undergrowth;
> Then took the other, as just as fair,
> And having perhaps the better claim,
> Because it was grassy and wanted wear;
> Though as for that the passing there
> Had worn them really about the same,
> And both that morning equally lay
> In leaves no step had trodden back.
> Oh, I kept the first for another day!
> Yet knowing how way leads on to way,
> I doubted if I should ever come back.
> I shall be telling this with a sigh
> Somewhere ages and ages hence:
> Two roads diverged in a wood, and I—
> I took the one less traveled by,
> And that has made all the difference.

Many of us take the road less travelled but in doing so create a path for those who will eventually follow, carrying our life as their talisman.

As for the poems we carry into this issue, Lynn Hoffman shares the passage of time in "Happy Birthday;" Victoria Boynton's "RD. Trip Gods" gives a new slant to road trips; "Ghosts and Illegals" by Lee Passarella and several more may just become your new favorites.

In our prose department, the *Things We Carry* ranges from the courage to see hope in the face of devastation ("Close to My Heart" by Gail Jeidy); the memory of ancestors and the tokens they've left behind ("Two Ancestors…" by Jeff Rasley); or perhaps it is to carry the truth we discover around us, "The Weight of Bearing Witness" by Erica L. Kaufman, which begins:

> "I remember the exact moment when I was in high school and realized that history books would never be able to tell us the whole story."

Amanda Wray, in "Black Dolls," explores the handmade dolls that were crafted, loved, and carried by her grandmother and passed on to her. "Constitution Ave," both photo and commentary by Brett Busang, records the day-to-day simple acts that renew and rebuild a neighborhood. "I Wasn't There" by John Poblocki carries the memory and causes of one man's suicide following Viet Nam, a story hardly fictional, and one that has sadly been repeated with each new war.

We are also pleased to present Rachel Routier's "Roots of Green," wherein a blind woman's interview invites us into a world filled with a full spectrum of color, texture, and the fantastic, asking the haunting question, "Tell me, traveler, what do you see?"

We, the editors, hope you enjoy the Things We Carry issue of *American Athenaeum* and in reading and pondering our selections of voices, that you may consider what you carry and more importantly, why.

Thank you and welcome to *American Athenaeum*

Jan Nerenberg, Prose Editor
Summertime, 2013

> To him whose elastic
> And vigorous thought
> Keeps pace with the sun,
> The day is a perpetual morning.
>
> —Henry Thoreau

⇒ *AMERICA TALKS*

THE WEIGHT OF BEARING WITNESS
by erica l. kaufman

I remember the exact moment when I was in high school and realized that history books would never be able to tell us the whole story.

We were taught about the Holocaust in school. We read a chapter in our textbooks; we watched *Schindler's List*. We learned about numbers, about facts and figures. We listened to the heart-wrenching stories of survivors. We were told that something awful happened. We were told the role that the rest of the world played in allowing it to happen. And, as Americans, we were shown the role the US played in ending the war and liberating the concentration camps.

But there are some things that we can never be told. There are some things that words can never truly convey. There are some things that photographs can't show us.

In 2007, while in college, I had the opportunity to visit Poland, and more specifically, the existing concentration camps through a program familiar to many Jewish youths called, Birthright Israel. Along with my sister, Bonnie, we ventured on what was known as the March of the Living, which started in the Warsaw ghetto, went through the remnants of Auschwitz and Majdanek, and finally ended with a stop in Israel. Birthright Israel exists to provide Jewish youths the opportunity to connect to Israel, to visit a place that they may otherwise have been unable to. The program exists to essentially pay tribute to, and remember those who perished during the Holocaust, to strengthen Jewish identity, and to prepare future Jews to bear witness.

Prior to arriving, I don't know if I truly prepared myself for what I would see in Poland. I read the brochures and pamphlets that detailed what I would see. I had spent time reading my textbooks, doing my homework. After all, being Jewish and having family in Poland during WWII, I had read more than the required reading for history class—I read nearly every book I could get my hands on, from autobiographies like Alicia Appleman-Jurman's *Alicia: My Story* or Elie Wiesel's *Night*, to fictional accounts like Lois

Things They Carry 11

Lowry's *Number the Stars,* and Jane Yolen's *The Devil's Arithmetic.* I saw the photos. I watched the movies. But in the end, having seen it—having stepped foot in a concentration camp—I don't know if I could say that there *would* have been a way to prepare.

The first stop on the trip took us to Auschwitz. My stomach churned as I walked in, on the same rock-laden dirt paths that had taken our relatives to their deaths. Once through the famous wrought-iron gate, it looked like I had imagined—historical and preserved. We walked on from the gate, across a vast expanse of field—green, tended to—past the remnants of once crowded barracks that sat scattered and empty in rows across the camp, like doppelgangers of each other. We walked past the crumbing brick structures that could have been the beginnings of something, but were really the endings; we were told they used to be gas chambers. We walked past fences laced across the top with coiled, rusted barbed wire. We walked past dusty glass boxes filled with relics—silverware, photographs, jewelry, items the Nazis had collected from their prisoners. Bonnie and I laced our fingers together and followed our group through the camp. It felt ghostly, or otherworldly—we were standing on ground that we knew only through the accounts of the survivors, on ground that most of us never thought we'd stand on. It seemed too poetic to talk about the fields of yellow flowers that we passed—bright, vibrant, lively. It seemed too poetic, even, to talk about how it felt like we were seeing everything through a black and white filter—the shadowy, looming fences creating a sense of negative space. I was seeing in real life what I had only viewed in pictures. It was emotional to consider what once happened under the same sky that we now stood under.

Majdanek was the second camp we visited and much harder. While Auschwitz was set up like a museum—plaques, signs, people working, relics behind glass cases—Majdanek, still technically a museum, was untouched in comparison. When you hear accounts of the Holocaust, you hear about Auschwitz, you hear about Buchenwald, you hear about Bergen-Belsen, but you hardly ever hear about Majdanek. (Just the fact that spellcheck recognizes "Auschwitz" but not "Majdanek" is interesting to me.) The word felt new in my mouth when we visited and I repeated it, "my-dahn-eck, my-dahn-eck."

When our group arrived, we were the only ones there, which added to the eerie stillness in the place. There were no plaques or signs or touristy things. In fact, it looked like it could have been liberated yesterday—it was not hard to imagine ghosts occupying the barracks with their clean wooden flooring and the grounds with their paths worn over from hundreds of feet taking them each day, not hard to imagine that people had been here, had only recently vacated, had slept in these barracks and been subjected to atrocities in these medical rooms. A single boulder, large and reminiscent of Sisyphus—and we were told that, yes, the Jews were forced to push this stone, back and forth, aimlessly, endlessly—rested at the top of the hill, as if waiting for its prisoner to return.

I could give you the statistics about Majdanek. I could tell you that it was considered a death camp, that it is now considered the most well-preserved of the concentration camps, that the number of Jewish people murdered there has been debated since the liberation of the camp in 1944, that Vladek Spiegelman, father of Art Spiegelman, the author of *Maus*, was a prisoner there. But you can read these facts in any book that mentions Majdanek.

What I can tell you is that the Majdanek in the history books doesn't come remotely close to the real thing. It's one thing to read about millions of people that were exterminated, and another thing entirely to see a crematorium and a gas chamber in real life. I remember feeling hot; the tour guides gave little information about what to expect at the end of the long dirt road that led to the camps. We walked and walked, seeing red rooftops peeking out far off in the horizon, saying nothing to each other. Then I saw it, grayish, pockmarked cement and big curving lines, a mausoleum. It held an enormous pile of ashes—ashes that continued on down lower, far below where we could see, and formed a large, circular structure that, from far away, looked almost like a spacecraft. Despite being closed for nearly seventy years, it felt like the ashes still permeated the air, felt like we could feel the ashes brushing our faces, settling on our skins, like a fine, translucent layer that we would never be able to wash off. The tour guide explained that the ashes were mixed with dirt and compost, which compacted them in the mausoleum and prevented them from blowing away entirely. In front of the mausoleum we prayed together—those of us unfamiliar with Hebrew stumbled over the words from the Mourners' Kaddish.

What I found myself most stunned and affected by was the closeness of the town to Majdanek. Books will tell you that while some concentration camps were in rural areas, Majdanek was unique in its proximity to a major city, Lublin. At the center of the camp, I *didn't* have to squint to make out the houses that surrounded it. I could practically see the people living in them, enjoying their backyards, feeding their children and animals, driving their cars to and from work and parking in their driveways, standing on their back porches and seeing their neighboring Jews being marched to off to death. I could imagine the townspeople witnessing what was going on—daily. They most certainly heard the cries; they heard the gunshots; they could see the smoke and smell the burning flesh in the air. The close proximity was unsettling, to see just how many people had to shut their eyes. They contributed to the injustice, either by actively participating, or by being a silent bystander. It's difficult to convey in words. You can say, "Majdanek was next to a major city." And then you visit and see that people worked in the tall buildings overlooking the camp, and you wonder, perhaps they even watched the prisoners on their lunch breaks, like some sort of gruesome reality television show.

And yet—even as I write this, you can read a similar story in books or on the Internet. But it's still important to *say* it, to remind people that Majdanek does not just exist in static, in photographs, but is still there, living, and breathing, and it *happened*.

This is the part of my life where it all became very real to me. It was real before, in the stories, but seeing it, it became a part of my reality.

It's been almost six years since I visited Majdanek. There is a sort of heaviness that comes from seeing the camps that stays with me. It's a heaviness laced with the knowledge that we are now in the unique position to not only share our experience with others, but the unique position in that we *must* be *able* to share our experiences. It's a heaviness that comes, at least partially, from feeling powerless and confused—how can I tell people what I saw? How can I convince people that this is something we cannot allow to exist only in textbooks, in a one-month unit at school? How can I do my part to make sure that people never forget? Our generation will see the last of the Holocaust survivors pass away—that is a fact. As the years go by and survivors grow older, we must be able to continue on the tradition of bearing witness in their place.

Not only will the survivors cease to exist, but the concentration camps are in varying stages of deterioration. (I saw this plainly during my visit). There are many opinions on what to do, with some believing that they should be preserved or restored, so that the structures can continue to bear witness to the atrocities of the Holocaust. Some people believe that the camps should be allowed to crumble—for how could anyone rebuild a place where such unspeakable things happened? Many survivors believe that if the camps are allowed to disintegrate, it will only make it that much easier for anti-Semitics to deny that the Holocaust ever happened in the first place. Still others say that because the Holocaust is such an incomprehensible event, a visit to the concentration camps will not make it any easier for people to understand.

It's hard to say with certainty what should be done. But I will say, as someone who feels strongly about my responsibility to bear witness, that I may never have been able to do just that without seeing the camps with my own eyes. And I think it is not something that can easily be denied to future youth—the opportunity to see a piece of the world that is very much our history and responsibility to keep alive.

I have talked to other Jewish youth, particularly to Bonnie, about what it actually means to *bear witness*. It can feel, at times, that we have nothing new to add to the large amount of writing that has already been done on the topic of the Holocaust. It is easy (for me) to feel as though my individual story does not make a difference. And in a way, that much is true. It is not my individual story that is important, but the overall *implications* of my story. As Jewish youth, as participants of the March of the Living program, as impassioned people who recognize the importance of keeping alive the stories of both the survivors and those who perished, we must make the effort to always, always bear witness.

Bearing witness is not just telling our stories and sharing our experiences. It comes in smaller actions too—by calling out people who think it's okay to make anti-Semitic jokes, by acknowledging Holocaust Remembrance Day, by encouraging other Jewish youth to go and witness the camps, to speak out against injustice and wrong information—because, yes, even though people find it hard to believe, there are still people out there who deny that the

Holocaust ever happened at all, and so on. Bearing witness, above all, is acknowledging that the weight we feel in our hearts is absolutely necessary in ensuring that nobody ever forgets what happened in the Warsaw Ghetto, in Auschwitz, in Majdanek. It is about recognizing that we share a common responsibility to remember, a responsibility that, at times, can feel overwhelming.

I am not a historian or a philosopher. I cannot tell you anything about facts and numbers and I cannot give any insight as to why it happened or answer any questions about what to do in the future. What I am is someone who has seen firsthand what it looked like in Poland during the war, and that now, in some small way, is attempting to bear witness.

⇒ *POETRY*

HAPPY BIRTHDAY
by Lynn Hoffman

The old man's muscles, vines
grown tight around a wrinkled trunk,
warning of a smaller crop,
promising richer, darker fruit.

"Having fun?" he said.
                  Well, I...
"Fun is good," he said.
"It's medicine against the romantics," he said.
"The romantics are like the shingles
or the vine louse," he said,
"They hurt like hell, they kill the root.
The romantics is worse than
the go-blutes, chillier than the chillblains.
You caught a cold,
you need the cure.
Have fun, fun is good." He said.
                  Do I know you?
"You will," he said,

"Happy Birthday"

ROAST CORN MAN
by Robert Truscott

            —*New York City streets, c. 1930*
I can't look at him
without change.
I asked him
for an ear.

Cheap joke.

He didn't understand
the words;
he reached inside
to bring out the corn.

He suspected nothing.
I moved as quickly
as I could,

telling him fields in Iowa
are endless as the dead;
rows and rows and rows
of martial silk and stalks
grew as he worked.

Passersby chatted,
read the news,
set the world straight;

the signs across
the street
sold men's clothes
that he could never buy.

I let him go,
and then,
before he could close
the lid,
I shot him.

GHOST AND ILLEGALS
by Lee Passarella

Driving in the suburbs and the exurbs
of Atlanta, I watch for them this April,
the ectoplasmic denizens of ancient burial grounds.

They festoon the sweet gums and loblollies,
trailing their purple winding sheets in the wind,
the ghostly evidence of past habitation.

Some clapboard farmhouse and barn sheltered
under those pines, when all of them were young,
from the baleful Cyclops eye of August. But April,

August, January, cycling through the many years,
have killed all evidence of place except the strangling vines,
the ghostly racemes of wisteria. Here and there

along the interstate, I see them haunting a white oak
in dangling clusters, sometimes mirrored upward
by the engorged nipples of an empress tree in bud,

erect with the purple urge of equinox: beautiful invasives
both, far from their Asian home, where memory
holds on to more than April ghosts among the oaks.

LIFELINES
by Shirley Kuo

you must know that when you are pressing
wordless promises into my palms i am reminded
of how my mother used to scrawl on the walls of
the house in black ink, meaningless scribbles that
transformed into the language of her heartbeat. she'd
tuck the lines next to the edges of the family photos
hooked on the living room wall, hide them behind the
bookshelf so my father would never see. it was only
after she died, after we began packing up boxes of her
possessions that he saw her lifelines etched in every

nook and cranny, loud as they were small: *look at me.*
look at me. i am alive. now, standing before you, i can
see the cracks carved along the ridges of your spine,
the path between your ribs. i can feel your nimble fingers,
fingers that have shredded daisy petals and yet cradled
the sun's rays. now i am telling you this: i see you.
i am looking at you. i recognize you.

RD. TRIP GODS by Victoria Boynton

They call her Our Lady of the Rearview Mirror,
Saint Interstate complete with Bumper-sticker prayers.
And every day another Capital Letter.
She uses only nouns for You, god.
Or numbers. Or case-sensitive passwords.
So many Menu gods to choose from:
Here at the shrine of the No Thank You god,
she keeps tissues in the dashboard cupholder
and prays to the Windshield Wiper No-Crying god
and the god of Carwash Waterproofing
and the god of Signage and of Tuneups.
They call her Our Lady of the Rearview Mirror
in Love's Truck Stop, squatting like a bunker
in the Tennessee dark.
She's faithful to the god of Fast-Food Condiments,
squeezing You out of a thousand tiny tubes,
smearing You on her face and over her arms,
never forgetting the backs of her knees.
On the highway, You ride her bumper, crouched,
peering in, then drinking out of the tailpipe.
Could You be the god of Roadkill or of Mood Disorders?
Our Lady of the Rearview Mirror loves You
Crypto-god and Car god with Bling,
Speed Trap god, frilled in Burger King wrappers,
Big-belly Pothole god in clanking muffler necklaces,
Shed god, stripping the edge of things,
Or Shred god swaying in a wig of tire scrap.
Are You a roadside Kali of eggs and home-fries,
stealing bits off a greasy plate,
Your sacrament, an emergency snack-pack
in the trunk with the flairs?
Our Lady of the Rearview Mirror loves You so much
that she stomps on the gas,
copying Your ecstatic speed
until she hears the Apocalyptic Sirens of Mr. State Police god
here to save her.
She rolls down her window filled with gratitude for His attentions
and awaits His word.

SOKUSHINBUTSU
by Duke Trott

Buddhist Self-Mummification

A bell rings from my grave through out the day,
so the mourners keep their yellow flowers.
When will my soul escape my life's decay?

To keep thoughts of mortal pleasure away
I sit in lotus for the final hours.
A bell rings from my grave through out the day

I ate only to keep hunger at bay,
little is left for time to devour.
When will my soul escape my life's decay?

My final occupation is to pray
that I may transcend the cosmic tower.
A bell rights from my grave through out the day.

A life of suffering is what we pay
to enter into its source of power.
When will my soul escape my life's decay?

My soul was forged as I followed The Way
a soul now open, for God to scour.
A bell rings from my grave through out the day.
When will my soul escape my life's decay?

SITALA: SHE WHO MAKES COOL
Excerpted from *Under the Nimba Tree*
by Berwyn Moore

Village in the Terai, 1953—*At her shrines, Sitala, the goddess of smallpox, is depicted in red, sitting on a lotus leaf and holding nimba leaves in her four hands. Villagers make daily offerings to her, and the dangerously ill are placed in front of her image where they wait for a cure and often die.*
—George Moore

                She arrived in *chitra*,
the hot season. Draped in red silk, she sat
atop an ass, under the nimba tree, broom
in one hand, a brass pot in the other, pale
skin smooth as opal. The stricken
crumpled before her, muttering puja,
pricking their boils with a thorn.

                Goddess of sores and pustules,
fever demon at her side, she possessed them
with the fiery breath of her favor: they were
blessed, her chosen vessels. They rubbed
her body and theirs with turmeric, offered
her chants and handfuls of cold rice.

                The doctor-sahib arrived,
coolies trailing, backpacks brimming
with antiseptic, vials, and bifurcated needles.
He smiled, squatted near a small girl, her cheeks
not yet pocked, knowing he could save her.
But the villagers shooed him away with sticks
and scruffy dogs, afraid he would anger
their beloved goddess, that she would withhold
her cooling touch. He showed them the clean
flesh of his back and hips and the small, round
crater on his shoulder, the coin-sized scar,
all that remained of the few pokes of a needle
years before. He explained *disease, vaccination,
immunity*, words for which there was no
translation. *Khe Garne*, his interpreter

shrugged—*what to do?*—and walked away.

                The doctor returned, a sadhu
leading, garish beads and matted coils of hair
and beard cascading across his saffron robe,
his face streaked in red and white paint.
The villagers hushed as the doctor unfurled
his poster, six-feet square, of Sitala, clad
in her royal red, sitting on a lotus leaf.
This time she held in her four hands syringes
and vials of vaccine, the man to her left,
snubbing her plea for a needle and plunging
headlong into a funeral pyre, the man to her right,
baring his arm for the needle, then smiling,
suddenly plump and rich, a black topi
on his head, a fat purse in his hand.

                The clerics, Buddhist
and Hindu, lined up first, then every man,
woman, and child, those yet unmarked
by Sitala's fiery baptism, ambled, quiet
and reverent, to the doctor's ready hands.
They brought him figs and lychee. They
bowed as to a god, this one tall and pale.
He jabbed each arm, once, then twice,
until the drop of serum appeared, and Sitala,
placated, withdrew her blistering grip.

THE COST OF WAR
by Major Chris Heatherly

I was not always this way.
The soldier who left for Iraq and Afghanistan
Was not the same that returned.
The battlefields followed me home;
They get lost at the bottom of a whiskey bottle.
At least for a while.
Small things take me back
A sound, a smell, and I am there again
In the moment... And it feels so impossibly real.
Sweating through my body armor
Tight grip on my rifle
Tight grip on the lives in my trust
Returning home
 I live in the now
The here
The present
Do not ask me to feel shame for what I did
I do not.
Or offer pity.
Politicians take heed:
Not all wounds are visible,
Look too closely and you may not like what you see.
Losing grip on reality.
Losing grip on life.
Scar tissue my armor against the world.
Think about the human cost
Before you send us to fight again
Because our battle starts at the end of your war.

⇒ VIEWS FROM THE PAST

THE BURNING OF OUR HOUSE
Copied on loose paper, July 10th, 1666
by Anne Bradstreet (1612–72)

In silent night when rest I took,
For sorrow neer I did not look,
I wakened was with thundring nois
And Piteous shreiks of dreadfull voice.
That fearful sound of fire and fire,
Let no man know is my Desire.
I, starting up, the light did spye,
And to my God my heart did cry
To strengthen me in my Distresse
And not to leave me succourlesse.
Then coming out beheld a space,
The flame consume my dwelling place.

And, when I could no longer look,
I blest his Name that gave and took,
That layd my goods now in the dust:
Yea, so it was, and so 'twas just.
It was his own: it was not mine;
Far be it that I should repine.

He might of All justly bereft,
But yet sufficient for us left.
When by the Ruines oft I past,
My sorrowing eyes aside did cast,
And here and there the places spye
Where oft I sate, and long did lye.

Here stood that Trunk, and there that chest;
There lay that store I counted best:
My pleasant things in ashes lye,
And them behold no more shall I.
Under thy roof no guest shall sitt,
Nor at thy Table eat a bitt.

Things They Carry 26

No pleasant tale shall 'ere be told,
Nor things recounted done of old.
No Candle 'ere shall shine in Thee,
Nor bridegroom's voice ere heard shall bee.
In silence ever shalt thou lye;
Adieu, Adeiu; All's vanity.

Then straight I gin my heart to chide,
And didst thy wealth on earth abide?
Didst fix thy hope on mouldring dust,
The arm of flesh didst make thy trust?
Raise up thy thoughts above the skye
That dunghill mists away may flie.

Thou hast an house on high erect
Fram'd by that mighty Architect,
With glory richly furnished,
Stands permanent tho' this bee fled.
It's purchased, and paid for too
By him who hath enough to doe.

A Prise so vast as is unknown,
Yet, by his Gift, is made thine own.
There's wealth enough, I need no more;
Farewell my Pelf, farewell my Store.
The world no longer let me Love,
My hope and Treasure lyes Above.

INVICTUS
by William Ernest Henley (1849–1903)

Out of the night that covers me,
Black as the pit from pole to pole,
I thank whatever gods may be
For my unconquerable soul.

In the fell clutch of circumstance
I have not winced nor cried aloud.
Under the bludgeonings of chance
 My head is bloody, but unbowed.

Beyond this place of wrath and tears
Looms but the Horror of the shade,
And yet the menace of the years
Finds and shall find me unafraid.

It matters not how strait the gate,
How charged with punishments the scroll.
I am the master of my fate:
I am the captain of my soul.

TEWA SONG OF THE SKY LOOM
by Anonymous

Oh our Mother the Earth, oh our Father the Sky!
Your children are we, and with tired backs
We bring you the gifts that you love.
Then weave for us a garment of brightness;
May the warp be the white light of morning,
May the weft be the red light of evening,
May the fringes be the falling rain,
May the border be the standing rainbow.
Thus weave for us a garment of brightness
That we may walk fittingly where birds sing,
That we may walk fittingly where grass is green
Oh our Mother the Earth, oh our Father the Sky!

VIETNAMESE FOLK POEM
by Anonymous

The twelfth moon for potato growing,
the first for beans, the second for eggplant.
In the third, we break the land
to plant the rice, in the fourth while the rains are strong.
The man ploughs, the woman plants,
and in the fifth comes the harvest, and the gods are good—
an acre yields five full baskets this year.
I grind and pound the paddy, strew husks to cover the
    manure,
and feed the hogs with bran.
Next year, if the land is fruitful,
I shall pay the taxes for you.
In plenty or in want, there will still be me and you,
always the two of us.
Isn't that better than prospering alone?

THE NEW COLOSSUS
by Emma Lazarus (1849–87)

Not like the brazen giant of Greek fame
With conquering limbs astride from land to land;
Here at our sea-washed, sunset gates shall stand
A mighty woman with a torch, whose flame
is the imprisoned lightning, and her name
Mother of Exiles. From her beacon-hand
Glows worldwide welcome; her mild eyes command
The air-bridged harbor that twin cities frame,
"Keep, ancient lands, your storied pomp!" cries she
With silent lips. "Give me your tired, your poor,
Your huddled masses yearning to breathe free,
The wretched refuse of your teeming shore,
Send these, the homeless, tempest-tossed to me,
I lift my lamp beside the golden door!"

THE FIRST TELEPHONE CALL
by Alexander Grahame Bell (1847–1922)
Transcribed by Hunter Liguore

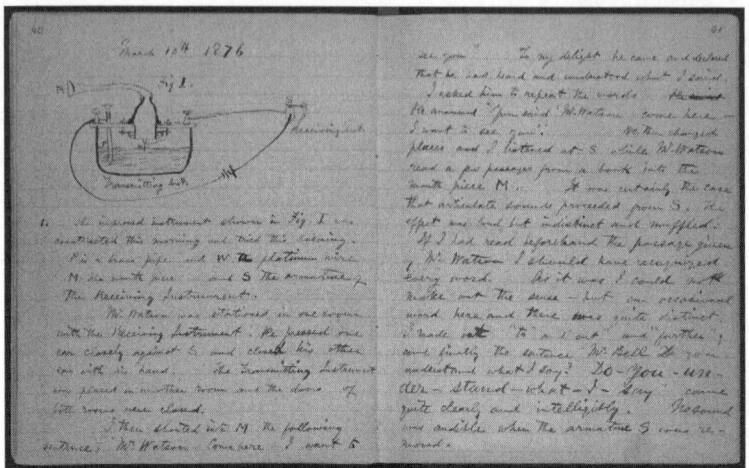

Bell's journal showing diagram of first telephone.
(Image courtesy of the Bell Family Papers)

March 10, 1896

The instrument shown in Fig. I was constructed this morning and tried this evening. **P** is a brass pipe, and **W** platinum wire; **M** is the mouthpiece and **S** is the armature of the receiving instrument.

Mr. Watson was stationed in one room with the receiving instrument. He pressed an ear closely against S and closed his other ear with his hand. The transmitting instrument was placed in another room and the doors of both rooms were closed.
I then shouted into M the following sentence: "Mr. Watson—come here—I want to see you."

To my delight he came and declared that he had heard and understood what I said. I asked him to repeat the words. He answered, "You said, 'Mr. Watson—come here—I want to see you.'"

We then exchanged places and I listened at S while Mr. Watson read a few passages from a book into the mouthpiece.

It was certainly the case that articulate sounds proceeded from S. The effect was loud but indistinct and muffled. If I had read

Things They Carry 32

beforehand the passage given by Mr. Watson, I should have recognized every word.

As it was, I could not make out the sense, but an occasional word here and there was quite distinct. I made out "to" and "out" and "further" and finally the sentence, "Mr. Bell, do you understand what I say?"

"Do-You-Un-der-stand-What-I-Say" came quite clearly and intelligibly. No sound was audible when the armature S was removed.

THE CYCLONE
by Frank L. Baum (1856–1919)

Dorothy lived in the midst of the great Kansas prairies, with Uncle Henry, who was a farmer, and Aunt Em, who was the farmer's wife. Their house was small, for the lumber to build it had to be carried by wagon many miles. There were four walls, a floor and a roof, which made one room; and this room contained a rusty looking cookstove, a cupboard for the dishes, a table, three or four chairs, and the beds. Uncle Henry and Aunt Em had a big bed in one corner, and Dorothy a little bed in another corner. There was no garret at all, and no cellar—except a small hole dug in the ground, called a cyclone cellar, where the family could go in case one of those great whirlwinds arose, mighty enough to crush any building in its path. It was reached by a trap door in the middle of the floor, from which a ladder led down into the small, dark hole.

When Dorothy stood in the doorway and looked around, she could see nothing but the great gray prairie on every side. Not a tree nor a house broke the broad sweep of flat country that reached to the edge of the sky in all directions. The sun had baked the plowed land into a gray mass, with little cracks running through it. Even the grass was not green, for the sun had burned the tops of the long blades until they were the same gray color to be seen everywhere. Once the house had been painted, but the sun blistered the paint and the rains washed it away, and now the house was as dull and gray as everything else.

When Aunt Em came there to live she was a young, pretty wife. The sun and wind had changed her, too. They had taken the sparkle from her eyes and left them a sober gray; they had taken the red from her cheeks and lips, and they were gray also. She was thin and gaunt, and never smiled now. When Dorothy, who was an orphan, first came to her, Aunt Em had been so startled by the child's laughter that she would scream and press her hand upon her heart whenever Dorothy's merry voice reached her ears; and she still looked at the little girl with wonder that she could find anything to laugh at.

Uncle Henry never laughed. He worked hard from morning till night and did not know what joy was. He was gray also, from his long beard to his rough boots, and he looked stern and solemn, and rarely spoke.

It was Toto that made Dorothy laugh, and saved her from growing as gray as her other surroundings. Toto was not gray; he was a little black dog, with long silky hair and small black eyes that twinkled merrily on either side of his funny, wee nose. Toto played all day long, and Dorothy played with him, and loved him dearly.

Today, however, they were not playing. Uncle Henry sat upon the doorstep and looked anxiously at the sky, which was even grayer than usual. Dorothy stood in the door with Toto in her arms, and looked at the sky too. Aunt Em was washing the dishes.

From the far north they heard a low wail of the wind, and Uncle Henry and Dorothy could see where the long grass bowed in waves before the coming storm. There now came a sharp whistling in the air from the south, and as they turned their eyes that way they saw ripples in the grass coming from that direction also.

Suddenly Uncle Henry stood up.

"There's a cyclone coming, Em," he called to his wife. "I'll go look after the stock." Then he ran toward the sheds where the cows and horses were kept.

Aunt Em dropped her work and came to the door. One glance told her of the danger close at hand.

"Quick, Dorothy!" she screamed. "Run for the cellar!"

Toto jumped out of Dorothy's arms and hid under the bed, and the girl started to get him. Aunt Em, badly frightened, threw open the trap door in the floor and climbed down the ladder into the small, dark hole. Dorothy caught Toto at last and started to follow her aunt. When she was halfway across the room there came a great shriek from the wind, and the house shook so hard that she lost her footing and sat down suddenly upon the floor.

Then a strange thing happened.

The house whirled around two or three times and rose slowly through the air. Dorothy felt as if she were going up in a balloon.

The north and south winds met where the house stood, and made it the exact center of the cyclone. In the middle of a cyclone the air is generally still, but the great pressure of the wind on every side of the house raised it up higher and higher, until it was at the very top of the cyclone; and there it remained and was carried miles and miles away as easily as you could carry a feather.

It was very dark, and the wind howled horribly around her, but Dorothy found she was riding quite easily. After the first few whirls around, and one other time when the house tipped badly, she felt as if she were being rocked gently, like a baby in a cradle.

Toto did not like it. He ran about the room, now here, now there, barking loudly; but Dorothy sat quite still on the floor and waited to see what would happen.

Once Toto got too near the open trap door, and fell in; and at first the little girl thought she had lost him. But soon she saw one of his ears sticking up through the hole, for the strong pressure of the air was keeping him up so that he could not fall. She crept to the hole, caught Toto by the ear, and dragged him into the room again, afterward closing the trap door so that no more accidents could happen.

Hour after hour passed away, and slowly Dorothy got over her fright; but she felt quite lonely, and the wind shrieked so loudly all about her that she nearly became deaf. At first she had wondered if she would be dashed to pieces when the house fell again; but as the hours passed and nothing terrible happened, she stopped worrying and resolved to wait calmly and see what the future would bring. At last she crawled over the swaying floor to her bed, and lay down upon it; and Toto followed and lay down beside her.

In spite of the swaying of the house and the wailing of the wind, Dorothy soon closed her eyes and fell fast asleep.

WHAT TO A SLAVE, IS THE FOURTH OF JULY?
Delivered in Rochester, New York, July 4, 1852
by Frederick Douglass (1817–95)

Fellow citizens, pardon me, and allow me to ask, why am I called upon to speak here today? What have I, or those I represent, to do with your national independence? Are the great principles of political freedom and of natural justice, embodied in that Declaration of Independence, extended to us? And am I, therefore, called upon to bring our humble offering to the national altar, and to confess the benefits, and express devout gratitude for the blessings resulting from your independence to us?

Would to God, both for your sakes and ours, that an affirmative answer could be truthfully returned to these questions. Then would my task be light, and my burden easy and delightful. For who is there so cold that a nation's sympathy could not warm him? Who so obdurate and dead to the claims of gratitude, that would not thankfully acknowledge such priceless benefits? Who so stolid and selfish that would not give his voice to swell the hallelujahs of a nation's jubilee, when the chains of servitude had been torn from his limbs? I am not that man. In a case like that, the dumb might eloquently speak, and the "lame man leap as an hart."

But such is not the state of the case. I say it with a sad sense of disparity between us. I am not included within the pale of this glorious anniversary! Your high independence only reveals the immeasurable distance between us. The blessings in which you this day rejoice are not enjoyed in common. The rich inheritance of justice, liberty, prosperity, and independence, bequeathed by your fathers, is shared by you, not by me. The sunlight that brought life and healing to you has brought stripes and death to me. This Fourth of July is yours, not mine. You may rejoice, I must mourn. To drag a man in fetters into the grand illuminated temple of liberty, and call upon him to join you in joyous anthems, were inhuman mockery and sacrilegious irony. Do you mean, citizens, to mock me, by asking me to speak today? If so, there is a parallel to your conduct. And let me warn you, that it is dangerous to copy the example of a nation [Babylon] whose crimes, towering up to heaven, were thrown down by the breath of the Almighty, burying that nation in irrecoverable ruin.

Fellow citizens, above your national, tumultuous joy, I hear the mournful wail of millions, whose chains, heavy and grievous yesterday, are today rendered more intolerable by the jubilant shouts that reach them. If I do forget, if I do not remember those bleeding children of sorrow this day, "may my right hand forget her cunning, and may my tongue cleave to the roof of my mouth!"

To forget them, to pass lightly over their wrongs and to chime in with the popular theme would be treason most scandalous and shocking, and would make me a reproach before God and the world.

My subject, then, fellow citizens, is "American Slavery." I shall see this day and its popular characteristics from the slave's point of view. Standing here, identified with the American bondman, making his wrongs mine, I do not hesitate to declare, with all my soul, that the character and conduct of this nation never looked blacker to me than on this Fourth of July.

Whether we turn to the declarations of the past, or to the professions of the present, the conduct of the nation seems equally hideous and revolting. America is false to the past, false to the present, and solemnly binds herself to be false to the future. Standing with God and the crushed and bleeding slave on this occasion, I will, in the name of humanity, which is outraged, in the name of liberty, which is fettered, in the name of the Constitution and the Bible, which are disregarded and trampled upon, dare to call in question and to denounce, with all the emphasis I can command, everything that serves to perpetuate slavery -- the great sin and shame of America! "I will not equivocate - I will not excuse." I will use the severest language I can command, and yet not one word shall escape me that any man, whose judgment is not blinded by prejudice, or who is not at heart a slave-holder, shall not confess to be right and just.

But I fancy I hear some of my audience say it is just in this circumstance that you and your brother Abolitionists fail to make a favorable impression on the public mind. Would you argue more and denounce less, would you persuade more and rebuke less, your cause would be much more likely to succeed. But, I submit, where all is plain there is nothing to be argued. What point in the anti-slavery creed would you have me argue? On what branch of the subject do the people of this country need light? Must I undertake to prove that the slave is a man? That point is conceded already. Nobody doubts it. The slaveholders themselves acknowledge it in the enactment of laws for their government. They acknowledge it when they punish disobedience on the part of the slave. There are seventy-two crimes in the State of Virginia, which, if committed by a black man (no matter how ignorant he be), subject him to the punishment of death; while only two of these same crimes will subject a white man to like punishment.

What is this but the acknowledgment that the slave is a moral, intellectual, and responsible being? The manhood of the slave is conceded. It is admitted in the fact that Southern statute books are covered with enactments, forbidding, under severe fines and penalties, the teaching of the slave to read and write. When you can point to any such laws in reference to the beasts of the field, then I may consent to argue the manhood of the slave. When the dogs in your streets, when the fowls of the air, when the cattle on your hills, when the fish of the sea, and the reptiles that crawl, shall be unable to distinguish the slave from a brute, then I will argue with you that the slave is a man!

For the present it is enough to affirm the equal manhood of the Negro race. Is it not astonishing that, while we are plowing, planting, and reaping, using all kinds of mechanical tools, erecting houses, constructing bridges, building ships, working in metals of brass, iron, copper, silver, and gold; that while we are reading, writing, and ciphering, acting as clerks, merchants, and secretaries, having among us lawyers, doctors, ministers, poets, authors, editors, orators, and teachers; that we are engaged in all the enterprises common to other men—digging gold in California, capturing the whale in the Pacific, feeding sheep and cattle on the hillside, living, moving, acting, thinking, planning, living in families as husbands, wives, and children, and above all, confessing and worshipping the Christian God, and looking hopefully for life and immortality beyond the grave—we are called upon to prove that we are men?

Would you have me argue that man is entitled to liberty? That he is the rightful owner of his own body? You have already declared it. Must I argue the wrongfulness of slavery? Is that a question for republicans? Is it to be settled by the rules of logic and argumentation, as a matter beset with great difficulty, involving a doubtful application of the principle of justice, hard to understand? How should I look today in the presence of Americans, dividing and subdividing a discourse, to show that men have a natural right to freedom, speaking of it relatively and positively, negatively and affirmatively? To do so would be to make myself ridiculous, and to offer an insult to your understanding. There is not a man beneath the canopy of heaven who does not know that slavery is wrong for him.

What! Am I to argue that it is wrong to make men brutes, to rob them of their liberty, to work them without wages, to keep them ignorant of their relations to their fellow men, to beat them with sticks, to flay their flesh with the lash, to load their limbs with irons, to hunt them with dogs, to sell them at auction, to sunder their families, to knock out their teeth, to burn their flesh, to starve them into obedience and submission to their masters? Must I argue that a system thus marked with blood and stained with pollution is wrong? No—I will not. I have better employment for my time and strength than such arguments would imply.

What, then, remains to be argued? Is it that slavery is not divine; that God did not establish it; that our doctors of divinity are mistaken? There is blasphemy in the thought. That which is inhuman cannot be divine. Who can reason on such a proposition? They that can, may—I cannot. The time for such argument is past.

At a time like this, scorching irony, not convincing argument, is needed. Oh! had I the ability, and could I reach the nation's ear, I would today pour out a fiery stream of biting ridicule, blasting reproach, withering sarcasm, and stern rebuke. For it is not light that is needed, but fire; it is not the gentle shower, but thunder. We need the storm, the whirlwind, and the earthquake. The feeling of the nation must be quickened; the conscience of the nation must be roused; the propriety of the nation must be startled; the hypocrisy of the nation must be exposed; and its crimes against God and man must be denounced.

What to the American slave is your Fourth of July? I answer, a day that reveals to him more than all other days of the year, the gross injustice and cruelty to which he is the constant victim. To him your celebration is a sham; your boasted liberty an unholy license; your national greatness, swelling vanity; your sounds of rejoicing are empty and heartless; your shouts of liberty and equality, hollow mock; your prayers and hymns, your sermons and thanksgivings, with all your religious parade and solemnity, are to him mere bombast, fraud, deception, impiety, and hypocrisy - a thin veil to cover up crimes which would disgrace a nation of

Things They Carry 40

savages. There is not a nation of the earth guilty of practices more shocking and bloody than are the people of these United States at this very hour.

Go search where you will, roam through all the monarchies and despotisms of the Old World, travel through South America, search out every abuse and when you have found the last, lay your facts by the side of the everyday practices of this nation, and you will say with me that, for revolting barbarity and shameless hypocrisy, America reigns without a rival.

MEDITATIONS
by Marcus Aurelius (121–80 CE)

Begin the morning by saying to yourself, I shall meet with the busybody, the ungrateful, arrogant, deceitful, envious, unsocial. All these things happen to them by reason of their ignorance of what is good and evil. But I who have seen the nature of the good that it is beautiful, and of the bad that it is ugly, and the nature of him who does wrong, that it is akin to me, not only of the same blood or seed, but that it participates in the same intelligence and the same portion of the divinity, I can neither be injured by any of them, for no one can fix on me what is ugly, nor can I be angry with my kinsman, nor hate him, For we are made for cooperation, like feet, like hands, like eyelids, like the rows of the upper and lower teeth. To act against one another then is contrary to nature; and it is acting against one another to be vexed and to turn away.

Whatever this is that I am, it is a little flesh and breath, and the ruling part. Throw away thy books; no longer distract thyself: it is not allowed; but as if you were now dying, despise the flesh; it is blood and bones and a network, a contexture of nerves, veins, and arteries. See the breath also, what kind of a thing it is, air, and not always the same, but every moment sent out and again sucked in. The third then is the ruling part: consider thus: Thou art an old man; no longer let this be a slave, no longer be pulled by the strings like a puppet to unsocial movements, no longer either be dissatisfied with thy present lot, or shrink from the future.

All that is from the gods is full of Providence. That which is from fortune is not separated from nature or without an interweaving and involution with the things which are ordered by Providence. From thence all things flow; and there is besides necessity, and that which is for the advantage of the whole universe, of which thou art a part. But that is good for every part of nature which the nature of the whole brings, and what serves to maintain this nature. Now the universe is preserved, as by the changes of the elements so by the changes of things compounded of the elements. Let these principles be enough for thee, let them always be fixed opinions. But cast away the thirst after books, that you may not die murmuring, but cheerfully, truly, and from thy heart thankful to the gods.

Things They Carry 42

Remember how long thou hast been putting off these things, and how often thou hast received an opportunity from the gods, and yet dost not use it. Thou must now at last perceive of what universe thou art a part, and of what administrator of the universe thy existence is an efflux, and that a limit of time is fixed for thee, which if thou dost not use for clearing away the clouds from thy mind, it will go and thou wilt go, and it will never return.

Every moment think steadily as a Roman and a man to do what thou hast in hand with perfect and simple dignity, and feeling of affection, and freedom, and justice; and to give thyself relief from all other thoughts. And thou wilt give thyself relief, if thou doest every act of thy life as if it were the last, laying aside all carelessness and passionate aversion from the commands of reason, and all hypocrisy, and self-love, and discontent with the portion which has been given to thee. You see how few the things are, the which if a man lays hold of, he is able to live a life which flows in quiet, and is like the existence of the gods; for the gods on their part will require nothing more from him who observes these things.

Do wrong to thyself, do wrong to thyself, my soul; but thou wilt no longer have the opportunity of honoring thyself. Every man's life is sufficient. But thine is nearly finished, though thy soul reverences not itself but places thy felicity in the souls of others.

Do the things external which fall upon thee distract thee? Give thyself time to learn something new and good, and cease to be whirled around. But then thou must also avoid being carried about the other way. For those too are triflers who have wearied themselves in life by their activity, and yet have no object to which to direct every movement, and, in a word, all their thoughts.

Through not observing what is in the mind of another a man has seldom been seen to be unhappy; but those who do not observe the movements of their own minds must of necessity be unhappy.

This thou must always bear in mind, what is the nature of the whole, and what is my nature, and how this is related to that, and what kind of a part it is of what kind of a whole; and that there is no one who hinders thee from always doing and saying the things which are according to the nature of which thou art a part.

Theophrastus, in his comparison of bad acts—such a comparison as one would make in accordance with the common notions of mankind- says, like a true philosopher, that the offences

Things They Carry 43

which are committed through desire are more blameable than those which are committed through anger. For he who is excited by anger seems to turn away from reason with a certain pain and unconscious contraction; but he who offends through desire, being overpowered by pleasure, seems to be in a manner more intemperate and more womanish in his offences. Rightly then, and in a way worthy of philosophy, he said that the offence which is committed with pleasure is more blameable than that which is committed with pain; and on the whole the one is more like a person who has been first wronged and through pain is compelled to be angry; but the other is moved by his own impulse to do wrong, being carried towards doing something by desire.

Since it is possible that thou may depart from life this very moment, regulate every act and thought accordingly. But to go away from among men, if there are gods, is not a thing to be afraid of, for the gods will not involve thee in evil; but if indeed they do not exist, or if they have no concern about human affairs, what is it to me to live in a universe devoid of gods or devoid of Providence? But in truth they do exist, and they do care for human things, and they have put all the means in man's power to enable him not to fall into real evils. And as to the rest, if there was anything evil, they would have provided for this also, that it should be altogether in a man's power not to fall into it. Now that which does not make a man worse, how can it make a man's life worse? But neither through ignorance, nor having the knowledge, but not the power to guard against or correct these things, is it possible that the nature of the universe has overlooked them; nor is it possible that it has made so great a mistake, either through want of power or want of skill, that good and evil should happen indiscriminately to the good and the bad. But death certainly, and life, honor and dishonor, pain and pleasure, all these things equally happen to good men and bad, being things which make us neither better nor worse. Therefore they are neither good nor evil.

How quickly all things disappear, in the universe the bodies themselves, but in time the remembrance of them; what is the nature of all sensible things, and particularly those which attract with the bait of pleasure or terrify by pain, or are noised abroad by vapory fame; how worthless, and contemptible, and sordid, and perishable, and dead they are- all this it is the part of the intellectual faculty to observe. To observe too who these are whose opinions and voices give reputation; what death is, and the fact that, if a man looks at it in itself, and by the abstractive power of reflection resolves into their parts all the things which present themselves to the imagination in it, he will then consider it to be nothing else than an operation of nature; and if any one is afraid of an operation of nature, he is a child. This, however, is not only an operation of nature, but it is also a thing which conduces to the purposes of nature. To observe too how man comes near to the deity, and by what part of him, and when this part of man is so disposed.

Nothing is more wretched than a man who traverses everything in a round, and pries into the things beneath the earth, as the poet says, and seeks by conjecture what is in the minds of his neighbors, without perceiving that it is sufficient to attend to the daemon within him, and to reverence it sincerely. And reverence of the daemon consists in keeping it pure from passion and thoughtlessness, and dissatisfaction with what comes from gods and men. For the things from the gods merit veneration for their excellence; and the things from men should be dear to us by reason of kinship; and sometimes even, in a manner, they move our pity by reason of men's ignorance of good and bad; this defect being not less than that which deprives us of the power of distinguishing things that are white and black.

Though you should be going to live three thousand years, and as many times ten thousand years, still remember that no man loses any other life than this which he now lives, nor lives any other than this which he now loses. The longest and shortest are thus brought to the same. For the present is the same to all, though that which perishes is not the same; and so that which is lost appears to be a mere moment. For a man cannot lose either the past or the future: for what a man has not, how can any one take this from him? These two things then thou must bear in mind; the one, that all things from eternity are of like forms and come round in a circle, and that it makes no difference whether a man shall see the same things during a hundred years or two hundred, or an infinite time; and the second, that the longest liver and he who will die soonest lose just the same. For the present is the only thing of which a man can be deprived, if it is true that this is the only thing which he has, and that a man cannot lose a thing if he has it not.

Remember that all is opinion. For what was said by the Cynic Monimus is manifest: and manifest too is the use of what was said, if a man receives what may be got out of it as far as it is true.

The soul of man does violence to itself, first of all, when it becomes an abscess and, as it were, a tumor on the universe, so far as it can. For to be vexed at anything which happens is a separation of ourselves from nature, in some part of which the natures of all other things are contained. In the next place, the soul does violence to itself when it turns away from any man, or even moves towards him with the intention of injuring, such as are the souls of those who are angry. In the third place, the soul does violence to itself when it is overpowered by pleasure or by pain. Fourthly, when it plays a part, and does or says anything insincerely and untruly. Fifthly, when it allows any act of its own and any movement to be without an aim, and does anything thoughtlessly and without considering what it is, it being right that even the smallest things be done with reference to an end; and the end of rational animals is to follow the reason and the law of the most ancient city and polity.

Of human life the time is a point, and the substance is in a flux, and the perception dull, and the composition of the whole body subject to putrefaction, and the soul a whirl, and fortune hard to divine, and fame a thing devoid of judgment. And, to say all in a word, everything which belongs to the body is a stream, and what belongs to the soul is a dream and vapor, and life is a warfare and a stranger's sojourn, and after-fame is oblivion. What then is that which is able to conduct a man? One thing and only one, philosophy. But this consists in keeping the daemon within a man free from violence and unharmed, superior to pains and pleasures, doing nothing without purpose, nor yet falsely and with hypocrisy, not feeling the need of another man's doing or not doing anything; and besides, accepting all that happens, and all that is allotted, as coming from thence, wherever it is, from whence he himself came; and, finally, waiting for death with a cheerful mind, as being nothing else than a dissolution of the elements of which every living being is compounded. But if there is no harm to the elements themselves in each continually changing into another, why should a man have any apprehension about the change and dissolution of all the elements? For it is according to nature, and nothing is evil which is according to nature.

WHAT IS AN AMERICAN?
From *Letters from an American Farmer*
by Hector St. John de Crevecoeur

I wish I could be acquainted with the feelings and thoughts which must agitate the heart and present themselves to the mind of an enlightened Englishman, when he first lands on this continent. He must greatly rejoice that he lived at a time to see this fair country discovered and settled; he must necessarily feel a share of national pride, when he views the chain of settlements which embellishes these extended shores. When he says to himself, this is the work of my countrymen, who, when convulsed by factions, afflicted by a variety of miseries and wants, restless and impatient, took refuge here. They brought along with them their national genius, to which they principally owe what liberty they enjoy, and what substance they possess. Here he sees the industry of his native country displayed in a new manner, and traces in their works the embryos of all the arts, sciences, and ingenuity which nourish in Europe. Here he beholds fair cities, substantial villages, extensive fields, an immense country filled with decent houses, good roads, orchards, meadows, and bridges, where an hundred years ago all was wild, woody, and uncultivated! What a train of pleasing ideas this fair spectacle must suggest; it is a prospect which must inspire a good citizen with the most heartfelt pleasure. The difficulty consists in the manner of viewing so extensive a scene. He is arrived on a new continent; a modern society offers itself to his contemplation, different from what he had hitherto seen. It is not composed, as in Europe, of great lords who possess everything, and of a herd of people who have nothing. Here are no aristocratical families, no courts, no kings, no bishops, no ecclesiastical dominion, no invisible power giving to a few a very visible one; no great manufacturers employing thousands, no great refinements of luxury. The rich and the poor are not so far removed from each other as they are in Europe. Some few towns excepted, we are all tillers of the earth, from Nova Scotia to West Florida. We are a people of cultivators, scattered over an immense territory, communicating with each other by means of good roads and navigable rivers, united by the silken bands of mild government, all respecting the laws, without dreading their power, because they are equitable. We are all animated with the spirit of an industry which is unfettered and unrestrained, because each person works for himself. If he travels through our rural districts he views not the hostile castle, and the haughty mansion, contrasted with the clay—built hut and miserable cabin, where cattle and men help to keep each other warm, and dwell in meanness, smoke, and indigence. A pleasing uniformity of decent competence appears throughout our habitations. The meanest of our log-houses is a dry and comfortable habitation.

Lawyer or merchant are the fairest titles our towns afford; that of a farmer is the only appellation of the rural inhabitants of our country. It must take some time ere he can reconcile himself to our dictionary, which is but short in words of dignity, and names of honor. There, on a Sunday, he sees a congregation of respectable farmers and their wives, all clad in neat homespun, well mounted, or riding in their own humble wagons. There is not among them an esquire, saving the unlettered magistrate. There he sees a parson as simple as his flock, a farmer who does not riot on the labor of others. We have no princes, for whom we toil, starve, and bleed: we are the most perfect society now existing in the world. Here man is <u>free</u> as he ought to be; nor is this pleasing equality so transitory as many others are. Many ages will not see the shores of our great lakes replenished with inland nations, nor the unknown bounds of North America entirely peopled. Who can tell how far it extends? Who can tell the millions of men whom it will feed and contain? for no European foot has as yet travelled half the extent of this mighty continent!

The next wish of this traveler will be to know whence came all these people? They are a mixture of English, Scotch, Irish, French, Dutch, Germans, and Swedes. From this promiscuous breed, that race now called Americans have arisen. The eastern provinces must indeed be excepted, as being the unmixed descendants of Englishmen. I have heard many wish that they had been more intermixed also: for my part, I am no wisher, and think it much better as it has happened. They exhibit a most conspicuous figure in this great and variegated picture; they too enter for a great share in the pleasing perspective displayed in these thirteen provinces. I know it is fashionable to reflect on them, but I respect them for what they have done; for the accuracy and wisdom with which they have settled their territory; for the decency of their manners; for their early love of letters; their ancient college, the first in this

Things They Carry 48

hemisphere; for their industry; which to me who am but a farmer, is the criterion of everything. There never was a people, situated as they are, who with so ungrateful a soil have done more in so short a time. Do you think that the monarchical ingredients which are more prevalent in other governments, have purged them from all foul stains? Their histories assert the contrary.

In this great American asylum, the poor of Europe have by some means met together, and in consequence of various causes; to what purpose should they ask one another what countrymen they are? Alas, two thirds of them had no country. Can a wretch who wanders about, who works and starves, whose life is a continual scene of sore affliction or pinching penury; can that man call England or any other kingdom his country? A country that had no bread for him, whose fields procured him no harvest, who met with nothing but the frowns of the rich, the severity of the laws, with jails and punishments; who owned not a single foot of the extensive surface of this planet? No! urged by a variety of motives, here they came.

Every thing has tended to regenerate them; new laws, a new mode of living, a new social system; here they are become men: in Europe they were as so many useless plants, wanting vegetative mould, and refreshing showers; they withered, and were mowed down by want, hunger, and war; but now by the power of transplantation, like all other plants they have taken root and flourished! Formerly they were not numbered in any civil lists of their country, except in those of the poor; here they rank as citizens. By what invisible power has this surprising metamorphosis been performed? By that of the laws and that of their industry. The laws, the indulgent laws, protect them as they arrive, stamping on them the symbol of adoption; they receive ample rewards for their labors; these accumulated rewards procure them lands; those lands confer on them the title of freemen, and to that title every benefit is affixed which men can possibly require. This is the great operation daily performed by our laws. From whence proceed these laws? From our government. Whence the government? It is derived from the original genius and strong desire of the people ratified and confirmed by the crown. This is the great chain which links us all, this is the picture which every province exhibits, Nova Scotia excepted.

There the crown has done all; either there were no people who had genius, or it was not much attended to: the consequence is, that the province is very thinly inhabited indeed; the power of the crown in conjunction with the musketos has prevented men from settling there. Yet some parts of it flourished once, and it contained a mild harmless set of people. But for the fault of a few leaders, the whole were banished. The greatest political error the crown ever committed in America, was to cut off men from a country which wanted nothing but men!

What attachment can a poor European emigrant have for a country where he had nothing? The knowledge of the language, the love of a few kindred as poor as himself, were the only cords that tied him: his country is now that which gives him land, bread, protection, and consequence: *Ubi panis ibi patria*, is the motto of all emigrants. What then is the American, this new man? He is either a European, or the descendant of a European, hence that strange mixture of blood, which you will find in no other country. I could point out to you a family whose grandfather was an Englishman, whose wife was Dutch, whose son married a French woman, and whose present four sons have now four wives of different nations.

He is an American, who, leaving behind him all his ancient prejudices and manners, receives new ones from the new mode of life he has embraced, the new government he obeys, and the new rank he holds. He becomes an American by being received in the broad lap of our great Alma Mater. Here individuals of all nations are melted into a new race of men, whose labors and posterity will one day cause great changes in the world. Americans are the western pilgrims, who are carrying along with them that great mass of arts, sciences, vigor, and industry which began long since in the east; they will finish the great circle.

The Americans were once scattered all over Europe; here they are incorporated into one of the finest systems of population which has ever appeared, and which will hereafter become distinct by the power of the different climates they inhabit. The American ought therefore to love this country much better than that wherein either he or his forefathers were born. Here the rewards of his industry follow with equal steps the progress of his labor; his labor is founded on the basis of nature, SELF-INTEREST: can it want a stronger allurement? Wives and children, who before in vain demanded of him a morsel of bread, now, fat and frolicsome, gladly help their father to clear those fields whence exuberant crops are to arise to feed and to clothe them all; without any part being claimed, either by a despotic prince, a rich abbot, or a mighty lord. Here religion demands but little of him; a small voluntary salary to the minister, and gratitude to God; can he refuse these? The American is a new man, who acts upon new principles; he must therefore entertain new ideas, and form new opinions. From involuntary idleness, servile dependence, penury, and useless labor, he has passed to toils of a very different nature, rewarded by ample subsistence.—This is an American.

SUMMER DAYS AT MOUNT SHASTA
by John Muir (1838-1914)

Standing on the edge of the Strawberry Meadows in the sundays of summer, not a foot or feather or leaf seems to stir; and the grand, towering mountain with all its inhabitants appears in rest, calm as a star. Yet how profound is the energy ever in action, and how great is the multitude of claws and teeth, wings and eyes, wide-awake and at work and shining! Going into the blessed wilderness, the blood of the plants throbbing beneath the life-giving sunshine seems to be heard and felt; plant growth goes on before our eyes, and every tree and bush and flower is seen as a hive of restless industry. The deeps of the sky are mottled with singing wings of every color and tone—clouds of brilliant chrysididae dancing and swirling in joyous rhythm, golden-barred vespidae, butterflies, grating cicadas and jolly rattling grasshoppers—fairly enameling the light, and shaking all the air into music. Happy fellows they are, every one of them, blowing tiny pipe and trumpet, plodding and prancing, at work or at play.

Though winter holds the summit, Shasta in summer is mostly a massy, bossy mound of flowers colored like the alpenglow that flushes the snow. There are miles of wild roses, pink bells of huckleberry and sweet manzanita, every bell a honey-cup, plants that tell of the north and of the south; tall nodding lilies, the crimson sarcodes, rhododendron, cassiope, and blessed linnaea; phlox, calycanthus, plum, cherry, crataegus, spiraea, mints, and clovers in endless variety; ivesia, larkspur, and columbine; golden aplopappus, linosyris, bahia, wyethia, arnica, brodiaea, etc.,—making sheets and beds of light edgings of bloom in lavish abundance for the myriads of the air dependent on their bounty.

The common honeybees, gone wild in this sweet wilderness, gather tons of honey into the hollows of the trees and rocks, clambering eagerly through bramble and hucklebloom, shaking the clustered bells of the generous manzanita, now humming aloft among polleny willows and firs, now down on the ashy ground among small gilias and buttercups, and anon plunging into banks of snowy cherry and buckthorn. They consider the lilies and roll into them, pushing their blunt polleny faces against them like babies on their mother's bosom; and fondly, too, with eternal love does Mother Nature clasp her small bee-babies and suckle them, multitudes at once, on her warm Shasta breast. Besides the common honeybee there are many others here, fine, burly, mossy fellows, such as were nourished on the mountains many a flowery century before the advent of the domestic species—bumblebees, mason-bees, carpenter-bees, and leaf-cutters. Butterflies, too, and moths of every size and pattern; some wide-winged like bats, flapping slowly and sailing in easy curves; others like small flying violets shaking about loosely in short zigzag flights close to the flowers, feasting in plenty night and day.

Deer in great abundance come to Shasta from the warmer foothills every spring to feed in the rich, cool pastures, and bring forth their young in the ceanothus tangles of the chaparral zone, retiring again before the snowstorms of winter, mostly to the southward and westward of the mountain. In like manner the wild sheep of the adjacent region seek the lofty inaccessible crags of the summit as the snow melts, and are driven down to the lower spurs and ridges where there is but little snow, to the north and east of Shasta.

Bears, too, roam this foodful wilderness, feeding on grass, clover, berries, nuts, ant eggs, fish, flesh, or fowl—whatever comes in their way—with but little troublesome discrimination. Sugar and honey they seem to like best of all, and they seek far to find the sweets; but when hard pushed by hunger they make out to gnaw a living from the bark of trees and rotten logs, and might almost live on clean lava alone.

Notwithstanding the California bears have had as yet but little experience with honeybees, they sometimes succeed in reaching the bountiful stores of these industrious gatherers and enjoy the feast with majestic relish. But most honeybees in search of a home are wise enough to make choice of a hollow in a living tree far from the ground, whenever such can be found. There they are pretty secure, for though the smaller brown and black bears climb well, they are unable to gnaw their way into strong hives, while compelled to exert themselves to keep from falling and at the same time endure the stings of the bees about the nose and eyes, without having their paws free to brush them off. But woe to the unfortunates who dwell in some prostrate trunk, and to the black bumblebees discovered in their mossy, mouse-like nests in the ground. With powerful teeth and claws these are speedily laid bare, and almost before time is given for a general buzz the bees, old and young, larvae, honey, stings, nest, and all, are devoured in one ravishing revel.

The antelope may still be found in considerable numbers to the northeastward of Shasta, but the elk, once abundant, have almost entirely gone from the region. The smaller animals, such as the wolf, the various foxes, wildcats, coon, squirrels, and the curious wood rat that builds large brush huts, abound in all the wilder places; and the beaver, otter, mink, etc., may still be found along the sources of the rivers. The blue grouse and mountain quail are plentiful in the woods and the sage-hen on the plains about the northern base of the mountain, while innumerable smaller birds enliven and sweeten every thicket and grove.

There are at least five classes of human inhabitants about the Shasta region: the Indians, now scattered, few in numbers and miserably demoralized, though still offering some rare specimens of savage manhood; miners and prospectors, found mostly to the north and west of the mountain, since the region about its base is overflowed with lava; cattle-raisers, mostly on the open plains to the northeastward and around the Klamath Lakes; hunters and trappers, where the woods and waters are wildest; and farmers, in Shasta Valley on the north side of the mountain, wheat, apples, melons, berries, all the best production of farm and garden growing and ripening there at the foot of the great white cone, which seems at times during changing storms ready to fall upon them—the most sublime farm scenery imaginable.

The Indians of the McCloud River that have come under my observation differ considerably in habits and features from the Diggers and other tribes of the foothills and plains, and also from the Pah Utes and Modocs. They live chiefly on salmon. They seem to be closely related to the Tlingits of Alaska, Washington, and Oregon, and may readily have found their way here by passing from stream to stream in which salmon abound. They have much better features than the Indians of the plains, and are rather wide-awake, speculative and ambitious in their way, and garrulous, like the natives of the northern coast.

Before the Modoc War they lived in dread of the Modocs, a tribe living about the Klamath Lake and the Lava Beds, who were in the habit of crossing the low Sierra divide past the base of Shasta on freebooting excursions, stealing wives, fish, and weapons from the Pitts and McClouds. Mothers would hush their children by telling them that the Modocs would catch them.

During my stay at the Government fish-hatching station on the McCloud I was accompanied in my walks along the riverbank by a McCloud boy about ten years of age, a bright, inquisitive fellow, who gave me the Indian names of the birds and plants that we met. The water-ousel he knew well and he seemed to like the sweet singer, which he called "Sussinny." He showed me how strips of the stems of the beautiful maidenhair fern were used to adorn baskets with handsome brown bands, and pointed out several plants good to eat, particularly the large saxifrage growing abundantly along the river margin. Once I rushed suddenly upon him to see if he would be frightened; but he unflinchingly held his ground, struck a grand heroic attitude, and shouted, "Me no fraid; me Modoc!"

Mount Shasta, so far as I have seen, has never been the home of Indians, not even their hunting ground to any great extent, above the lower slopes of the base. They are said to be afraid of fire-mountains and geyser basins as being the dwelling places of dangerously powerful and unmanageable gods. However, it is food and their relations to other tribes that mainly control the movements of Indians; and here their food was mostly on the lower slopes, with nothing except the wild sheep to tempt them higher. Even these were brought within reach without excessive climbing during the storms of winter.

On the north side of Shasta, near Sheep Rock, there is a long cavern, sloping to the northward, nearly a mile in length, thirty or forty feet wide, and fifty feet or more in height, regular in form and direction like a railroad tunnel, and probably formed by the flowing away of a current of lava after the hardening of the surface. At the mouth of this cave, where the light and shelter is good, I found many of the heads and horns of the wild sheep, and the remains of campfires, no doubt those of Indian hunters who in stormy weather had camped there and feasted after the fatigues of the chase. A wild picture that must have formed on a dark night—the glow of the fire, the circle of crouching savages around it seen through the smoke, the dead game, and the weird darkness and half-darkness of the walls of the cavern, a picture of cave-dwellers at home in the stone age!

Interest in hunting is almost universal, so deeply is it rooted as an inherited instinct ever ready to rise and make itself known. Fine scenery may not stir a fiber of mind or body, but how quick and how true is the excitement of the pursuit of game! Then up flames the slumbering volcano of ancient wildness, all that has been done by church and school through centuries of cultivation is for the moment destroyed, and the decent gentleman or devout saint becomes a howling, bloodthirsty, demented savage. It is not long since we all were cavemen and followed game for food as truly as wildcat or wolf, and the long repression of civilization seems to make the rebound to savage love of blood all the more violent. This frenzy, fortunately, does not last long in its most exaggerated form, and after a season of wildness refined gentlemen from cities are not more cruel than hunters and trappers who kill for a living.

Dwelling apart in the depths of the woods are the various kinds of mountaineers—hunters, prospectors, and the like—rare men, "queer characters," and well worth knowing. Their cabins are located with reference to game and the ledges to be examined, and are constructed almost as simply as those of the wood rats made of sticks laid across each other without compass or square. But they afford good shelter from storms, and so are "square" with the need of their builders. These men as a class are singularly fine in manners, though their faces may be scarred and rough like the bark of trees. On entering their cabins you will promptly be placed on your good behavior, and, your wants being perceived with quick insight, complete hospitality will be offered for body and mind to the extent of the larder.

These men know the mountains far and near, and their thousand voices, like the leaves of a book. They can tell where the deer may be found at any time of year or day, and what they are doing; and so of all the other furred and feathered people they meet in their walks; and they can send a thought to its mark as well as a bullet. The aims of such people are not always the highest, yet how brave and manly and clean are their lives compared with too many in crowded towns mildewed and dwarfed in disease and crime! How fine a chance is here to begin life anew in the free fountains and skylands of Shasta, where it is so easy to live and to die! The future of the hunter is likely to be a good one; no abrupt change about it, only a passing from wilderness to wilderness, from one high place to another.

Now that the railroad has been built up the Sacramento, everybody with money may go to Mount Shasta, the weak as well as the strong, fine-grained, succulent people, whose legs have never ripened, as well as sinewy mountaineers seasoned long in the weather. This, surely, is not the best way of going to the mountains, yet it is better than staying below. Many still small voices will not be heard in the noisy rush and din, suggestive of going to the sky in a chariot of fire or a whirlwind, as one is shot to the Shasta mark in a booming palace-car cartridge; up the rocky canyon, skimming the foaming river, above the level reaches, above the dashing spray—fine exhilarating translation, yet a pity to go so fast in a blur, where so much might be seen and enjoyed.

The mountains are fountains not only of rivers and fertile soil, but of men. Therefore we are all, in some sense, mountaineers, and going to the mountains is going home. Yet how many are doomed to toil in town shadows while the white mountains beckon all along the horizon! Up the canyon to Shasta would be a cure for all care. But many on arrival seem at a loss to know what to do with themselves, and seek shelter in the hotel, as if that were the Shasta they had come for. Others never leave the rail, content with the window views, and cling to the comforts of the sleeping car like blind mice to their mothers. Many are sick and have been dragged to the healing wilderness unwillingly for body-good alone. Were the parts of the human machine detachable like Yankee inventions, how strange would be the gatherings on the mountains of pieces of people out of repair!

How sadly unlike the whole-hearted ongoing of the seeker after gold is this partial, compulsory mountaineering!—as if the mountain treasuries contained nothing better than gold! Up the mountains they go, high-heeled and high-hatted, laden like Christian with mortifications and mortgages of divers sorts and degrees, some suffering from the sting of bad bargains, others exulting in good ones; hunters and fishermen with gun and rod and leggins; blithe and jolly troubadours to whom all Shasta is romance; poets singing their prayers; the weak and the strong, unable or unwilling to bear mental taxation. But, whatever the motive, all will be in some measure benefited. None may wholly escape the good of Nature, however imperfectly exposed to her blessings. The minister will not preach a perfectly flat and sedimentary sermon after climbing a snowy peak; and the fair play and tremendous impartiality of Nature, so tellingly displayed, will surely affect the after pleadings of the lawyer. Fresh air at least will get into everybody, and the cares of mere business will be quenched like the fires of a sinking ship.

Possibly a branch railroad may some time be built to the summit of Mount Shasta like the road on Mount Washington. In the mean time tourists are dropped at Sisson's, about twelve miles from the summit, whence as headquarters they radiate in every direction to the so-called "points of interest;" sauntering about the flowery fringes of the Strawberry Meadows, bathing in the balm of the woods, scrambling, fishing, hunting; riding about Castle Lake, the McCloud River, Soda Springs, Big Spring, deer pastures, and elsewhere. Some demand bears, and make excited inquiries concerning their haunts, how many there might be altogether on the mountain, and whether they are grizzly, brown, or black. Others shout, "Excelsior," and make off at once for the upper snowfields. Most, however, are content with comparatively level ground and moderate distances, gathering at the hotel every evening laden with trophies—great sheaves of flowers, cones of various trees, cedar and fir branches covered with yellow lichens, and possibly a fish or two, or quail, or grouse.

But the heads of deer, antelope, wild sheep, and bears are conspicuously rare or altogether wanting in tourist collections in the "paradise of hunters." There is a grand comparing of notes and adventures. Most are exhilarated and happy, though complaints may occasionally be heard. "The mountain does not look so very high after all, nor so very white; the snow is in patches like rags spread out to dry," reminding one of Sydney Smith's joke against Jeffrey, "D—n the Solar System; bad light, planets too indistinct." But far the greater number are in good spirits, showing the influence of holiday enjoyment and mountain air. Fresh roses come to cheeks that long have been pale, and sentiment often begins to blossom under the new inspiration.

The Shasta region may be reserved as a national park, with special reference to the preservation of its fine forests and game. This should by all means be done; but, as far as game is concerned, it is in little danger from tourists, notwithstanding many of them carry guns, and are in some sense hunters. Going in noisy groups, and with guns so shining, they are oftentimes confronted by inquisitive Douglas squirrels, and are thus given opportunities for shooting; but the larger animals retire at their approach and seldom are seen. Other gun people, too wise or too lifeless to make much noise, move slowly along the trails and about the open spots of the woods, like benumbed beetles in a snowdrift. Such hunters are themselves hunted by the animals, which in perfect safety follow them out of curiosity.

During the bright days of midsummer the ascent of Shasta is only a long, safe saunter, without fright or nerve strain, or even serious fatigue, to those in sound health. Setting out from Sisson's on horseback, accompanied by a guide leading a pack animal with provision, blankets, and other necessaries, you follow a trail that leads up to the edge of the timberline, where you camp for the night, eight or ten miles from the hotel, at an elevation of about ten thousand feet. The next day, rising early, you may push on to the summit and return to Sisson's. But it is better to spend more time in the enjoyment of the grand scenery on the summit and about the head of the Whitney Glacier, pass the second night in camp, and return to Sisson's on the third day.

The woods differ but little from those that clothe the mountains to the southward, the trees being slightly closer together and generally not quite so large, marking the incipient change from the open sunny forests of the Sierra to the dense damp forests of the northern coast, where a squirrel may travel in the branches of the thick-set trees hundreds of miles without touching the ground. Around the upper belt of the forest you may see gaps where the ground has been cleared by avalanches of snow, thousands of tons in weight, which, descending with grand rush and roar, brush the trees from their paths like so many fragile shrubs or grasses.

At first the ascent is very gradual. The mountain begins to leave the plain in slopes scarcely perceptible, measuring from two to three degrees. These are continued by easy gradations mile after mile all the way to the truncated, crumbling summit, where they attain a steepness of twenty to twenty-five degrees. The grand simplicity of these lines is partially interrupted on the north subordinate cone that rises from the side of the main cone about three thousand feet from the summit. This side cone, past which your way to the summit lies, was active after the breaking-up of the main ice-cap of the glacial period, as shown by the comparatively unwasted crater in which it terminates and by streams of fresh-looking, unglaciated lava that radiate from it as a center.

The main summit is about a mile and a half in diameter from southwest to northeast, and is nearly covered with snow and neve, bounded by crumbling peaks and ridges, among which we look in vain for any sure plan of an ancient crater. The extreme summit is situated on the southern end of a narrow ridge that bounds the general summit on the east. Viewed from the north, it appears as an irregular blunt point about ten feet high, and is fast disappearing before the stormy atmospheric action to which it is subjected.

At the base of the eastern ridge, just below the extreme summit, hot sulphurous gases and vapor escape with a hissing, bubbling noise from a fissure in the lava. Some of the many small vents cast up a spray of clear hot water, which falls back repeatedly until wasted in vapor. The steam and spray seem to be produced simply by melting snow coming in the way of the escaping gases, while the gases are evidently derived from the heated interior of the mountain, and may be regarded as the last feeble expression of the mighty power that lifted the entire mass of the mountain from the volcanic depths far below the surface of the plain.

The view from the summit in clear weather extends to an immense distance in every direction. Southeastward, the low volcanic portion of the Sierra is seen like a map, both flanks as well as the crater-dotted axis, as far as Lassen's Butte, a prominent landmark and an old volcano like Shasta, between ten and eleven thousand feet high, and distant about sixty miles. Some of the higher summit peaks near Independence Lake, one hundred and eighty miles away, are at times distinctly visible. Far to the north, in Oregon, the snowy volcanic cones of Mounts Pitt, Jefferson, and the Three Sisters rise in clear relief, like majestic monuments, above the dim dark sea of the northern woods. To the northeast lie the Rhett and Klamath Lakes, the Lava Beds, and a grand display of hill and mountain and gray rocky plains. The Scott, Siskiyou, and Trinity Mountains rise in long, compact waves to the west and southwest, and the valley of the Sacramento and the coast mountains, with their marvelous wealth of woods and waters, are seen; while close around the base of the mountain lie the beautiful Shasta Valley, Strawberry Valley, Huckleberry Valley, and many others, with the headwaters of the Shasta, Sacramento, and McCloud Rivers.

The Cinder Cone near Lassen's Butte is remarkable as being the scene of the most recent volcanic eruption in the range. It is a symmetrical truncated cone covered with gray cinders and ashes, with a regular crater in which a few pines an inch or two in

Things They Carry 60

diameter are growing. It stands between two small lakes which previous to the last eruption, when the cone was built, formed one lake. From near the base of the cone a flood of extremely rough black vesicular lava extends across what was once a portion of the bottom of the lake into the forest of yellow pine.

This lava flow seems to have been poured out during the same eruption that gave birth to the cone, cutting the lake in two, flowing a little way into the woods and overwhelming the trees in its way, the ends of some of the charred trunks still being visible, projecting from beneath the advanced snout of the flow where it came to rest; while the floor of the forest for miles around is so thickly strewn with loose cinders that walking is very fatiguing. The Pitt River Indians tell of a fearful time of darkness, probably due to this eruption, when the sky was filled with falling cinders which, as they thought, threatened every living creature with destruction, and say that when at length the sun appeared through the gloom it was red like blood.

Less recent craters in great numbers dot the adjacent region, some with lakes in their throats, some overgrown with trees, others nearly bare—telling monuments of Nature's mountain fires so often lighted throughout the northern Sierra. And, standing on the top of icy Shasta, the mightiest fire-monument of them all, we can hardly fail to look forward to the blare and glare of its next eruption and wonder whether it is nigh. Elsewhere men have planted gardens and vineyards in the craters of volcanoes quiescent for ages, and almost without warning have been hurled into the sky. More than a thousand years of profound calm have been known to intervene between two violent eruptions. Seventeen centuries intervened between two consecutive eruptions on the island of Ischia. Few volcanoes continue permanently in eruption. Like gigantic geysers, spouting hot stone instead of hot water, they work and sleep, and we have no sure means of knowing whether they are only sleeping or dead.

⇒ *ESSAYS*

LANGUAGE LESSONS
by Catherine Jagoe

When I first moved to the United States from England in 1986, I only planned to spend a year. Coming from a rural upbringing in the west Midlands, my knowledge of America was limited to episodes of the TV shows *Dallas, Starsky and Hutch,* and *The Virginian,* none of which offered any insights into life in Madison, Wisconsin, my destination. Even the word *Midwest* had layers of conflicting cultural meanings I was oblivious to—heartland, salt of the earth, flyover country, backwater. I made no preparations for culture shock. We shared a language, so how different could America really be?

When I arrived, it was summertime, which made it easy to fall in love with everything about my new surroundings: the huge, flawless blue skies, the warm weather, the space, the orderliness, the unexpected friendliness of the people, the biking, sailing, swimming, and running. Although Madison's size qualified it as a city, it seemed more like a vacation colony. There were no people in suits, no traffic jams, no obvious pollution. The airport parking lot was little more than a field. Most houses were built of wood instead of brick or stone, which to my eye made them seem temporary, like boathouses, not sturdy enough for human dwellings. People on campus dressed as if they were going to bed or the beach, in sweatpants, shorts and sandals.

Everything appeared larger, but also one-dimensional. Hardly any buildings were above two storeys high, and they did not seem deeply rooted. The main road, through the neighborhood where I lived, resembled a set for a western, as if the shop fronts were mere cardboard façades that could blow over in a strong wind. The sheer size of the land around us, the space that made that kind of horizontal, spread-out construction possible, overwhelmed me. In the countryside the fields were enormous; the eye was not bombarded with visual detail—hedgerows, winding lanes, trees, villages, undulations in the terrain—but encountered only flat earth and sky. What's more, you could drive for hours in any direction and nothing much changed. I had landed in an ocean of space.

American prosperity translated into larger sizes for everything—houses, cars, fridges, parking spaces, lakes, closets, salaries, roads and clothes. Popcorn was sold in places called *movie theaters* in buckets big enough for ten, not small paper bags, as I was used to. Work occupied a huge space in peoples' lives. Even emotions seemed super-sized. I wasn't sure why people smiled so widely; or why they said, "wow," as if seriously awed or impressed at what seemed like mundane remarks to me. I missed the deadpan humor and lightning-fast irony of British conversation, which seemed out of sync with the style of conversations here.

I moved into a little house on a lake, where I swam every day. The proximity to water and farmland felt reassuringly similar to my parents' home in Shropshire, which was a five-minute walk from a small mere, a canal and a farm. Soon, I was biking to campus to spend my days at the university library, stunned at the apparently limitless size of its collection, the fact that it was open at all hours, and that it allowed free access to the photocopy machines. (At Cambridge University, where I was a student, these were jealously guarded by the staff, who imposed a strict page limit for copies, demanded lengthy written requests, and charged exorbitant fees).

It was all very pleasant, but rather bewildering. I felt unmoored, at sea in a place where the language was familiar but altered, where even the simplest words could mean something different. What made it hard wasn't the new words like *eggplant* for aubergine or *zucchini* for courgette or *restroom* for toilets—I was a linguist, so I was used to learning new words—but the words that had retained the same spelling over the last four hundred years, while traveling divergent paths to new meanings. A *yard* was not made of concrete; *pants* were not underwear; *corn* was not wheat but maize; *chips* were not potato fries; *smart* did not mean well-dressed; a *brat* was not necessarily a nasty child. The language was studded with words with meanings that had shifted, either subtly or completely, such as *kettle, mad, produce, trunk, hockey, store, truck, candy, biscuit, football, holiday*, and *college*.

I kept thinking of the Venn diagrams learned in high school math, as word meanings expanded or shrank, so that a general category would become a subset or vice versa. For instance, the kind of thick, chilled custard called *pudding* here was certainly *a* pudding to a British speaker, but not to be confused with "pudding" the dessert course. For British speakers, *school* ends after

Things They Carry 63

high school, whereas for Americans it includes higher education, or indeed any form of learning, at any age. Some words depended on physical context. How to make my mother—thousands of miles away and confused about the six-hour time difference between us—understand what *winter* meant in Wisconsin? How to convey in one word the length and rigor of our five months of Siberian cold, blizzards, ice and sub-zero temperatures, when her experience of the word was England's gray, rainy forties and fifties? How to explain that a *muffin* was a jumbo-sized fairy cake and not something you toasted and ate with butter?

On an aside, the word *badger* caused me a peculiar cultural jolt. In a slightly uncanny coincidence, Wisconsin's official nickname, the *Badger State*, comes from the Cornishmen who came in the 1830s to mine for lead. Our family (also descended from Cornish tin miners) had a romance with badgers thanks to my naturalist father, who adored and revered them, and would spend long hours rambling the local woods every week noting recent activity in the dens, called *setts*, the locations of which he knew intimately. On summer nights he would sometimes post himself downwind and wait among the trees for hours, motionless, in hopes of a sighting. British badgers were the Eurasian variety; they looked and acted differently than their American cousins. They were tenacious fighters if cornered and tortured, (the verb "to badger" comes from the obsolete sport of badger-baiting), but otherwise were so shy, and extremely difficult to see. Even Mole and Rat have a hard time tracking down kindly old Mr. Badger in *The Wind in the Willows*. So I felt a visceral wrongness every time I saw the University of Wisconsin logo of a squat, pugnacious animal with its chest stuck out, the epitome of brash aggressiveness.

≈

G. B. Shaw wrote in *Pygmalion*, "the moment an Englishman opens his mouth, another Englishman despises him." The moment you open your mouth in Britain to say the simplest sentence, someone is reacting to you, putting you in a mental pigeonhole—my kind of person, not my kind of person. I grew up not being able to speak without apprehension of the results, which usually seemed to involve hostility or alienation. Arriving in Wisconsin for the first time, the idea that people might not instantly *dislike* me just for the way I spoke was a revelation. It made me realize how much

I braced for rejection every time I opened my mouth, how much pain and pronunciation were linked for me.

Linguistic anxiety was something I acquired in 1969, at the age of eight. My early childhood was spent in suburban Surrey, in the ambit of my parents, who spoke with a southeastern accent known as *Received Pronunciation* or *R.P.* (also known as the Queen's English or Oxford English.) Formerly a desirable and prestigious accent, R.P. was systematically inculcated for at least a hundred years at British *public schools* (meaning, a handful of the oldest and most exclusive private schools in Britain). In the age of empire, it made practical sense to erase regional accents among the ruling class, in order to make future colonial administrators more comprehensible to the subjects they would rule. My parents were good examples. My father was born to Irish parents in Kuala Lumpur, Malaya. My mother was born into an RAF family in what is now Pakistan, but at the time was known as the Northwest Frontier Province of India. My father had no trace of his parents' Irish accent because he had been sent to public school in England. His first job was a British government posting in northern Nigeria.

When my father said a sentence like, *she's been in the bath for half an hour*, he pronounced *bath* like *half,* and *hour* with the same long vowel /a:/. *Coffee* and *happy* were pronounced *coffi* and *happi*. The *u* in *revolution* was pronounced *revolyution*, not *revolootion*. The word *reduce* was pronounced *redyuce*, not *rejuice*.

I had no awareness of accent differences or discords while living in the south of England, although I'm sure I would have acquired it soon enough with age. My linguistic innocence ended abruptly, however, when we moved to a small town in Shropshire, on the Welsh border, and I began attending the local primary school. Suddenly, I had only to say one word, *hello*, for example, and children visibly reacted, withdrew, and mocked me as a snob. The old saying, "Sticks and stones may break my bones, but words can never hurt me," was certainly not true then. They perceived of my accent as *posh*, or a snobby, which sometimes led them to literally throw stones at me on the way home from school. An undercurrent of violence existed around language in British society that was never very far below the surface.

British people are more sensitive to accent than any other English-speaking country, because it is a mark of caste as well as geography. In the United Kingdom, (slightly smaller than the state

Things They Carry 65

of Oregon), regional accents are still vastly more different and various than they are in the United States in an area of comparable size. But people rarely ask each other, *where are you from?*, a question I encounter in America regularly. In the world where I grew up, the real question was: *are you one of us? Who are your people?* The answer was always instantly obvious from someone's accent—a remarkably accurate predictor of what kind of house you lived in, what kind of school you went to, and what your parents did.

In England in the '60s and '70s, locating someone geographically didn't matter as much as locating them socially in the class labyrinth. And class wasn't necessarily a reflection of income. My father was a teacher, my mother a secretary who left school at fourteen and became a housewife after she married. They had four children and money was very tight, yet they mixed with the staff at the local public school and the landed gentry, rather than the people who lived in the cottages on our street. In lifestyle, creed and habits, there was a gulf between us—something that the Shropshire children instantly perceived in my speech and resented.

Just as the children below me on the social ladder disliked me because they perceived me as privileged and condescending, I, in my turn, felt discomfort around the children of my parents' upper-class friends, because their accents conveyed a privileged existence—private school, skiing trips on the Continent, living in mansions—from which my family was permanently excluded because of income. With them, I felt awkward and ashamed in the homemade clothes my mother sewed; for me they were damning proof of our family's struggle to make ends meet.

British English is filled with shibboleths that can trip you up. You move gingerly, always aware of unexploded ordnance that might open up a gulf between *Us* and *Them*; between the people who say *napkin* and the people who say *serviette*; the people who say *tea* and the people who say *supper*; the people who say *sofa* and the people who say *settee*; the people who say *bye* and the people who say *ta-ta*.

Two decades after my move to America, I had an experience while on a visit to England that highlighted just how potent these shibboleths could be. While walking through a council estate in Cornwall, a group of young teenagers were hanging around, and I said hello to them. Instantly, they began parodying a rarefied, aristocratic accent—one only used now by the Queen and heard in

World War II newsreels—but they had picked up enough from those two syllables to detect that we weren't from the same social strata. Instinctively, they magnified the difference to grotesque, funhouse size, and wielded it as a weapon to mock me: "Eoh, helleoh, haa do you do?"

This kind of meanness and harassment was responsible for a whole generation of young people—my generation—adopting a different accent than their parents, one that didn't mark them either as working class or privileged, which allowed them to fit in better at school or work by concealing their class origins. For youngsters, like me, whose parents had R.P. accents, it involved toning them down, adopting many features of London working class usage and pronunciation in order to avoid arousing hostility. For example, deliberately using more glottal stops in place of the *t*: *sea'belt*, or *ne'work*. Pronouncing *tu* words, such as *Tuesday* or *tune*, as *chooseday* and *choon*. Or even shortening the *a* in words like *bath*. It also involved the use of more colloquial words and expressions, such as *cheers* for both thank you and goodbye. In my teens I was very aware of this linguistic chameleonism, and observed it in my siblings and peers, although we never spoke about it. We were trying to pass. In 1984, two years before I came to America, a linguist, David Rosewarne, identified this new phenomenon in the *Times Educational Supplement*, calling the new dialect, *Estuary English*, a term that stuck as the phenomenon expanded. Estuary English is now well on its way to becoming standard English across the class spectrum. Public figures as various as Prince Edward, David Beckham, and Jamie Oliver speak it; it's even now widespread at the BBC.

≈

Perhaps not surprisingly, given my crash course in the subtleties of accent, I showed an aptitude for languages as a teenager, and was accepted to study Modern Languages at Cambridge University in 1980, with funding from Shopshire County Council. However, I needed to study two modern languages, and I had only one, French. No beginners were accepted. You were expected to have a good grounding in both languages before you arrived. So in January 1980, at the age of nineteen, I left home for the first time to live in Madrid for six months as an au pair and pick up Spanish as best I could.

Things They Carry 67

In my new job, baffled by the strange customs, food, living arrangements, the move from a quiet backwater to a cacophonous capital city, and the stream of utterly incomprehensible speech that surrounded me every day, I went mute. I was terrified of both my employers and my charges, and wincingly afraid of making a mistake if I ventured beyond *Sí* and *No*, so I said as little as possible. Adult language learners don't have the advantages of children, who get a two-year grace period listening and observing before beginning to speak their first language. But I did my best to replicate it by keeping mostly silent for months; I kept copious notes of everything I heard and pored over them at night. I made a conscious effort to imitate whatever I heard, parroting phrases and reactions. Towards the end of my stay, even with my extremely limited vocabulary, people began remarking that I had a good accent.

As the years passed, my Spanish improved as I completed first an undergraduate and then a graduate degree in Spanish language and literature, and spent several spells living in Madrid. I realized that learning a foreign language allowed me to experiment with acquiring a new personality. In English I was a loner—reserved, cautious, ironic and misanthropic. In Spanish I was enthusiastic, friendly, outgoing and popular. I would chat about anything and everything just because I could, because it allowed me to practice sounding authentically Spanish.

Eventually, people in Spain stopped assuming I was foreign. My chameleon strategy had worked—I passed. Even when I was discovered to be English, they praised me for sounding so Spanish, for fitting in.

≈

When I moved to the United States, I couldn't use the strategy of accent imitation that worked so well for me in Spain. Doing so in my first language felt as if I would lose my core identity, and I couldn't create a middle ground like Estuary English, because I would be the sole speaker of a new dialect rather than part of a nationwide trend. It made sense to use the local lexicon, but changing my accent entirely from British to American was another matter. I had arrived as an adult, with a lifetime of speaking the language behind me, and to *deliberately* change, felt like a betrayal. In

Things They Carry 68

the bewilderment of a new environment, I needed the continuity of an identity with roots, even if they were somewhere else.

I made a parallel decision about my Spanish accent. My first academic job, in Illinois, involved teaching Spanish language, composition and literature in Spanish, which posed a set of linguistic challenges. My students' frame of reference was naturally Latin American, and generally Mexican; but by that point I had a firm linguistic identity in Spanish as a woman from Madrid. I didn't want to lose that identity, but wanted to meet my students and colleagues halfway. So I made the same adjustments I did to American English, using continent-specific words, but keeping my Madrid accent. I didn't use the Spanish pronoun system, or vocabulary that was only spoken in Spain. I had to develop bicultural fluency in Spanish as well as English, a working knowledge of Mexican Spanish (and that of other Latin American countries), without assuming it as an identity.

Accent loyalty was not without its drawbacks. In my first month here, I had to ask for a glass of *agua* in a restaurant because the waitress and I were unable to communicate over the word *water*—the long, flat British *a,* the soft *t* and the lack of *r*, combined to frustrate understanding. Interestingly, she had absolutely no problem understanding it in Spanish. Similarly, I was almost unable to make a reservation to fly to Newark because I couldn't make the phonetic difference between *Newark* and *New York* accurately enough to make sense to the increasingly irate airline sales rep on the other end of the phone.

Even now, a quarter-century later, with an American husband and son, I'm sometimes reluctant to make enquiries or place catalog orders over the phone for fear of not making myself understood. "You do it," I tell my husband, a New Yorker. "You speak the language." I still slightly dread having to spell our address out loud because our street name includes the word *lawn*, which always causes trouble. The *aw* vowel is much wider in American; in British English it is a smaller, rounder *o* sound. If pressed, Americans tend to write down *lone* when I say *lawn*.

In the early years there were frequent misunderstandings or slight bumps in communication. When my husband left me notes saying things like *I went to the store*, I would assume he was now somewhere else, or that it was from a different day altogether, because if he was still at the store he would've written *I've gone to the*

Things They Carry 69

store. British English uses the present perfect—*I have done*—to talk about the recent past.

Nowadays the differences I encounter between American and British are becoming ever subtler. A few years ago, I spent most of the day cooking a sumptuous meal for my father-in-law. Afterwards he sat back and said, "That was quite good." I was crushed, because for me *quite* was a detractor, not a re-enforcer. It was as if he had just said, "Well, that was passable."

≈

As Jonathan Raban, the author of *Driving Home,* puts it, when you're an immigrant, you need to "grow a memory." You lack all the shared allusions to culture and experience—characters from TV shows, minor political figures, advertising jingles, types of candy, names of athletes, sports, holidays and rituals, foods. I didn't know who Peewee Herman was, or what a Snickers bar was, or *hyperventilating*, or Woodstock, or *Friends*, or *90210*, or a *fourth down*, or a *strike*. I had no equivalent of a high school yearbook or a college roommate. I had never taken SATs or prelims. In the early years, I often felt lost or lonely in conversations because I had no companion memories to match those around me, effectively shutting me out from a community of experience.

Nowadays, I'm growing a memory through my son. I've lived in America for twenty-seven years, longer than any other place—half my life. I have a stake in the country now. I have given birth here. The foreign has become part of my family. As my son, with his American accent and vocabulary, goes through school I gradually acquire associations with each of the grades—riding the yellow school bus in kindergarten, learning to read in first grade, learning to ride a bike without training wheels in third grade, starting cursive in fourth grade. So far, my memory extends only to fifth grade; but in time, hopefully, I will vicariously experience the college system and young adulthood. At which point I will have caught up with myself, since I arrived at twenty-five. No longer simply a resident alien, I have *naturalized*. I may not sound like a native, but, like a bulb planted some place and left to its own devices, I have put down roots, multiplied, and settled in.

Things They Carry 70

TWO ANCESTORS AND TWO ANSWERS:
Where We Come From and Where Are We Going
Excerpted fr. *Pilgrimage: Sturgis to Wounded Knee & Back Home Again*
by Jeff Rasley

1.

One of my ancestors died as a result of the "action" at Wounded Knee on December 29, 1890. He was not among the hundreds of Sioux killed in what has come to be considered one of the worst atrocities in the history of the US military. He was one of the perpetrators, Lieutenant James Defrees Mann of the 7th US Cavalry.

In May of 1977, my mother, a journalist, wrote a story for our hometown newspaper, *The Goshen News*, published in May 1977, about our ancestor, Lt. Mann. My mom had learned about our ancestor when she was invited by the US military academy at West Point to represent the family at his "last roll call," which celebrates the one-hundredth anniversary of his graduation from West Point. My mom attended the ceremony, and later researched Lt. Mann's military career, which resulted in the article.

During a recent visit with my mom, while perusing the family scrapbook, I re-read the piece. It struck me as intriguing and even perverse to have an ancestor that most likely managed to get shot by friendly fire, especially since the Sioux weren't doing much shooting. My mother's article was a revelation for me when it was originally published in 1977, not just about our family history, but also about the history of Wounded Knee.

Re-reading my mom's article in the new millennium sparked enough interest that I did some further reading on Wounded Knee, including the 1970 best-selling book by Dee Brown, *Bury My Heart at Wounded Knee*. The book sheds light on the "Indian" perspective during the Removal Act years, which forced tribes from their ancestral land onto reservations starting in 1830, and consequently ended with the Battle of Wounded Knee. While the book was criticized for presenting chiefly the Native American point of view, for me, it seemed like it was time for an alternative view to the dominant US cavalry-centered story.

During the 1970s a sea of change occurred in the popular consciousness of Americans with respect to the treatment of Native Americans. The 1970 movie *Little Big Man*, based on the

1964 comic novel by Thomas Berger, and starring Dustin Hoffman, was wildly popular. For the first time, US cavalrymen were portrayed as the bad guys, and Native Americans as the good guys. Angst within the country about the Viet Nam War was at an all time high, and the movie contributed to it by comparing the way the US government treated Native Americans to the conduct of the war in Viet Nam.

Prior to the '70s, the prevailing view, supported by popular Western novels, TV shows, and movies, and especially textbooks, painted the indigenous tribes in a less than favorable fashion. During the 1960s, for instance, the idea that European settlers encountered "savages" was still being presented in American History classes taught in public and parochial schools, even though alternative histories existed and were available to scholars or those willing to confront conventional views. But it wasn't until the social, political, and cultural upheavals of the late 1960s that American popular consciousness was ready to consider history from the Native American perspective.

As a child in the late 1950s and '60s in a predominantly Caucasian town, my gang of neighborhood kids often played the game, Cowboys and Indians, where the "Indians" were always treated as the bad guys (just like in the history books). We took turns because we all wanted to be the John Wayne-like good guy, and wear our cowboy hats, and draw our six-shooters from the holsters to plug the war-painted "Injuns," just like in the movies. In those days, we were taught, "the only good Injun was a dead Injun." Where did kids in Goshen, Indiana get these ideas?

The kids in my neighborhood were mostly the descendants of small town Midwestern pioneers. The history we imbibed was that of the "winners" of the Indian Wars. If the "losers" had a history, we weren't exposed to it. However, change was afoot in the 1970s. A new narrative was developing.   Native Americans began to be portrayed in the popular media as wise and noble. A prime example is the character Big Chief in the movie, *One Flew over the Cuckoo's Nest*, an adaptation of Ken Kesey's 1962 novel. The novel did not make much of a splash, but the 1975 film directed by Miloš Forman won five Oscars and was hugely popular.

Another example was a commercial launched on the second Earth Day celebration in 1971 by the Keep America Beautiful campaign. The actor, Iron Eyes Cody, portrayed a Native

American shedding tears as a response to people littering. (The commercial shows a kid tossing out a wad of trash from a speeding car, which lands at Cody's feet.) The spot came to be known as "the Crying Indian," ad, and was an iconic representation in public service announcements shown on TV. Its winsomeness also helped the environmental movement gain popularity. However, it should be noted that Cody was actually Sicilian-American. In 1971 neither Hollywood nor Madison Avenue were yet ready to cast a Native American actor in a nationwide advertising campaign.

Although some of these representations of Native Americans in the popular media during the 1970s were excessively romanticized, they did start to reverse the negative images in the minds of people, like the kids I grew up with—the game eventually ran its course. Native Americans were finally being presented in popular forums in a positive light. America began to reconsider history form the Native point of view and to question their treatment by the US government.

There is no longer any dispute among historians that the "action" by the 7th US Cavalry at Wounded Knee was one of the worst of the many terrible events in the sad history of Native American encounters with US government forces in the nineteenth century. My mother's 1977 article summarized the accepted account of what happened at Wounded Knee. She described it as a massacre of "Indians." But her article also related our ancestor's version of the events.

While Lt. Mann lay dying from a gunshot wound after the Battle of Wounded Knee, a reporter from *Harper's Weekly* interviewed him. The *Harper's* article was reprinted in Lt. Mann's hometown newspaper, the *Goshen Democrat*, after the Lieutenant succumbed to his wound and died on January 15, 1891. My mother's 1977 article in *The Goshen News* summarized Lt. Mann's interview by the *Harper's* correspondent:

Lt. Mann was lying on his back with a bullet through his body. The young officer grew stern when he got to the critical part of his story. Lt. Mann said, "I saw three or four young bucks drop their blankets and I saw they were armed. Be ready to fire men," I said, "there is trouble." There was an instant and then we heard firing in the center of the Indians. "Fire," I shouted, and we poured it into them."

It is still unsettled as to who fired the first shot that started the battle. But as my mother's article explains, a gun accidentally went off while the Sioux were being disarmed by government troopers. Lt. Mann blamed "an old medicine man" for stirring up "the bucks." Although the Sioux were surrounded by heavily armed government forces, Lt. Mann claimed that the medicine man stoked defiance among the Sioux by telling them that they were invulnerable to the army's bullets because they wore "ghost shirts ... painted with magic symbols."

Whoever fired the first shot, the result was that federal soldiers killed around three hundred Sioux, mostly women and children.

2.

I have another story to share about a family connection with Native Americans. It involves a beaded vest that my great-great grandfather Valentine Berkey owned. I discovered the vest up in the attic when I was a kid. It was in an old chest, which looked like a pirate's treasure chest with metal ribs, a latch, and hump-backed top. It contained family artifacts my mother had received from deceased relatives. Things like Great-Aunt Caroline's button collection, hooked rugs made by my great-grandmother, Ella Mae, and pillowcases edged with tatting made by great-great aunt Ida.

My mother let me keep the vest, because I was so taken with it. The fabric on the front of the vest is tanned deerskin; the back panel is silky cloth. The front is covered with intricately beaded blooming flowers of various colors sewn onto the deerskin. It looks a lot like the vest Billy Bob Thornton wore playing Davy Crockett in the movie *The Alamo*.

The vest hung in my closet for several years. In high school I wore it a few times with hip-hugger bell-bottoms to parties. I thought it looked pretty cool when hippie styles were in. After the vest's few appearances as an accoutrement to my long hair and high-heel boots, it hung in the closet in my room for years, ignored.

After I married, my wife, Alicia, and I eventually removed some of my treasured childhood items from my old room. She was quite taken with the vest when she discovered it. So we packed it up and took it along with other childhood mementos, like my plastic model of *The Mummy*; a skeleton hand liberated from an anatomy lab at Goshen College; and an antique music box my grandmother gave me. Alicia later asked that same grandmother what she knew about the history of the vest.

Ouise (pronounced Weezie) told Alicia that her grandfather, Valentine Berkey, had owned a general store in Goshen. He did some trading with a Pottawattamie family, the last tribe left in the Goshen area. During a hard winter, Grandfather Berkey extended credit to them; his generosity helped them to avoid starving or removal to a reservation. The Pottawattamie people gave him the vest as a token of their appreciation. In doing some more research, I learned this through the Goshen Historical Society:

Things They Carry 75

"Valentine Berkey came to Elkhart County in the 1850s from his home state of Pennsylvania. Berkey served on the county council and was a deacon at the West Goshen Church of the Brethren, among other duties. He built his house, which sits immediately to the west of the Brethren church on Berkey Avenue. Berkey died in 1920 in California while visiting one of his children."

In the 1880s, while Lt. Mann fought the Sioux in the Black Hills, Valentine Berkey was trading with the last of the Pottawattamie in the Goshen area. Valentine may have had the kind of relationship with his tribal neighbors that I have been advocating through the Basa Village Foundation for the Rai people who live in the Nepal Himalayas.

Valentine must have been a man who valued community as he was deeply involved in his own. He served as a county councilman and church deacon. Valentine would have encountered a variety of other cultures and people in his trip to California before his death in 1920. So, he probably had an interest in expanding his understanding of other peoples and cultures. He must have had friendly relations with the Pottawattamie, since he traded with them and they honored him with the gift of the vest. One can imagine Valentine and his Pottawattamie friends sharing stories and tobacco on his front porch or outside his store.

I'm a lot like my great-great grandfather, in that I also value involvement with my local community. I serve on several nonprofit boards, lead a class at the Indianapolis First Friends Quaker Meeting, and serve as president of the Basa Village Foundation. I'm guessing Valentine and I would probably agree on how to live a good life.

Lt. Mann, on the other hand, went off to the West for the adventure of fighting a war on the frontier with an alien culture. (Imagine what guts that took!) He did not choose the staid life of a small town merchant. I'm guessing he yearned for adventure—and found it—as a soldier on the western frontier. Adventure *is* something I can relate with. The truth is, I have something in common with both of them.

As a kid growing up in Goshen, Indiana, I looked forward to and expected to serve in the US military. My adolescent opposition to the Viet Nam War changed that. I was lucky to receive a high lottery number for the Draft and was not called to serve. Instead, I did my adventuring hitchhiking around the country and across

Europe, riding a motorcycle down through Mexico, solo-kayaking across the Palau Island chain, and climbing and trekking the Himalayas. I have *invaded* other lands as a tourist-adventure traveler, and by my presence have contributed to the spread of the dominant Western culture. Wherever I have lived and traveled, I polluted the land with the leavings of my consumer culture. I haven't killed others, as Lt. Mann presumably did during his thirteen years of fighting Native Americans, but he probably lived closer to—and left a smaller footprint on—the natural world than I have. In no way, am I in a position to judge James Defrees Mann.

But I do part ways with him, when it comes to relating to people of a foreign culture, as the enemy, rather than potential friend, brother or sister. My friends in Basa call me "dhai", older brother, or "bhai," younger brother. I respond likewise, and call the grandmothers, "aamaa," and the grandfathers, "babu." We do not recognize being "other," or alien, or enemy. We encounter each other as friends and family.

Because, the truth is *we* and *all things* do come from the same source. If it all began with God—or whatever your name for it may be—then all of us, and all things, are of God. Where is this synergistic force taking our universe, world, and species? We don't know. But, as to sharing a common spirit, or origin, the Sioux had it right, and the Rai of Basa Village have it right. The old wisdom, which predates all the organized religions, holds that there is original spirit in everything in our universe. It does not recognize original sin as an inescapable condition of human being. It *does* recognize that we are all related through common origins.

We should live with each other as friends, brothers and sisters, and in harmony with all of nature. We do all come from the same source.

BLACK DOLLS
by Amanda Wray

On the morning of Thanksgiving, while my partner and I rushed around the kitchen readying dinner, my eleven-year-old niece posed a joke: "What's black and white and scary?" I took pause, and my partner bumped into my suddenly still body. Water aimed for boiling sloshed out of my grandmother's soup kettle and down the front of my apron. My niece waited. I didn't know what came next, but I anticipated that the punch line involved race. I tried to think quickly so that I could deflect this conversation. My sister and her husband were just then carrying their bags in for an overnight stay.

"A zebra with a lonely stripe," I said a bit too loud.

"Nooo," she sung back to me. "Michael Jackson." She slapped her leg and laughed boldly into the kitchen.

My sister stopped, two duffle bags heavy with clothes in one hand and a can of coconut milk in the other. I could hear my parents fussing about something in shushed voices over her shoulder, and she made eye contact with me. I was tempted to reciprocate her smile, just so the uncomfortable silence between us would pass. I wanted to dismiss this opportunity as too inconvenient to talk to my niece about race. Understanding race—conceptualizing it as something visible and invisible, constructed and lived, beyond "like" and "not like me" binaries—that process takes time. A lifetime.

I rested a gaze on my niece. "Would you tell that joke in front of a black person?"

She thought about it. "No," the smile gone from her face.

My sister said, "I told you Aunt Amanda wouldn't like that."

I turned to the Yukon Gold potatoes, drained and steaming, and I began mashing them with the antique tool from our first Thanksgiving in Tucson. In silence, I wondered a moment too long about the "that" in my sister's sentence. Did "that" signify the joke, as in Aunt Amanda doesn't like jokes? Or, did my sister see the superficial way the punch line treated race? Did she take issue with "black" being named as something scary and to be laughed at? Did she appreciate the pattern and the legacy of such a pattern? Or, was she just hiding behind a nondescript relative pronoun trying to calm my storm?

Things They Carry 78

"Why do those two ways of talking exist?" I asked the whole room. "I mean, why should we feel okay saying something around whites that we wouldn't say in front of people of different races?"

I reached into the refrigerator for butter, and I saw my niece glance down at her feet. "I'm not trying to make you feel guilty," I tried to reassure.

After a few minutes, she said, "I never thought about that" and walked out of the kitchen.

During my childhood, black dolls sewn by my grandmother's hand sat conspicuously on shelves and freshly made beds throughout our house. All other aspects of my 1980s, small-town Kentucky existence were white, which made the presence of black dolls around our house seem especially strange. Fewer than fifteen students of color attended my elementary and junior high schools, though I'm sure I'm misremembering and making invisible individuals. I called only one, a black girl named Jones, friend. We met in sixth grade and were among a class of 340 graduating seniors. We played sports together, and we both had working moms. Jones and I spent much of our freshman year discovering alcohol and abusing the independence provided by working class parents. Other than Jones, my neighborhood, my church, my Girl Scout group, our family friends, my doctor and dentist and the woman who cut our hair, were all white.

When I was five, I received two black dolls, one boy and one girl, and the next year I received two white dolls, again, a boy and a girl. I infrequently played with dolls, preferring cars and building cities to dressing up babies. Even when I played with dolls, I rarely chose the handmade ones because they required hand washing. My arthritic grandmother had stitched their clothes so painstakingly that I never took them out of the house.

The black dolls wore brimmed hats and gathered bonnets. Grandma sewed puffy bloomers that reached down past the knees of boys and girls. White aprons draped down the front of the girls' dresses and shirtless overalls covered the boys' black chests. The doll clothes were kept immaculate and ironed. Their red lips were sewn wide into a smile, and they were shoeless. Knotted segments of black and brown yarn were tied around each doll's head, and I remember twisting one knot so frequently that the stitches pulled out. My black doll, a few years old by then, was left bald on one side, and I felt so ashamed for having ruined my grandmother's work.

In comparison, the white dolls wore equally crisp church clothes: blue checkered dresses that hid white bloomers or black linen overalls that stretched tightly over button up flannel shirts. Flowing yellow-yarn-hair or pinned brown curls, smooth and unknotted, sat atop their heads. Unlike the black dolls, the white dolls sported black, hard-soled shoes with laces, and they smiled with pink lips.

Until I started high school, the dolls lived most of their time in an antique baby carriage in my room. When my friends came over, though, I stuffed the black dolls into my closet. I didn't know what having black dolls would convey to guests. I worried they might think I was trying to make fun of black people or that I wanted to be a black person. I didn't have a good reason for owning black dolls, except that they were a gift from my grandmother. It seemed rude to shush her work up in the closet, but it also seemed wrong to put it on display.

When my mother was just a toddler, my grandmother sewed everything by hand. Her stitches were less than a quarter of an inch: small, neat, and strong. She was regularly commissioned by others to alter clothes and to make quilts. Patterns of double wedding ring, Dutch baskets, and broken dishes warmed every bed. When someone married or had a baby, Grandma made a quilt. The last ten years, she made pillows, her arthritis too crippling to allow for quilting.

In 1955, the year the Supreme Court ruled school segregation unconstitutional, Grandma started making dolls. Long before the city high school was forced to integrate in 1956, poverty and rural remoteness dictated that all county students attended primary school together. The poor black and white kids, including my father, worked together on farms, ate lunch together in their one room schoolhouses, and interacted more peacefully than dominant narratives about the rural south usually represent. Conflict centered in town, but by 1963, my mother said racial animosity wasn't "talked about" anymore; the white students just ignored the black students and that somehow indicated harmony. The stories we tell construct our reality.

I tried to imagine that Grandma's black dolls were used to raise critical consciousness about changing race relations in the small

Things They Carry 80

town. Grandma's small town rested less than an hour from the Tennessee border, and she told me stories on several occasions that celebrated the hard work and criticized the unfair treatment of blacks. But, she also told me once that black folks smelled differently from whites. Like so many, Grandma masked her prejudice in socially polite ways, leaking it out behind closed doors among all whites. My love for this woman was intense. I respected her and I wanted to be like her, but I wanted her to be a feminist and activist. I wanted to forget her prejudices.

The town my mother grew up in is one she remembered as self-segregated: whites lived wherever they wanted and blacks lived on Marrowbone Hill. Far-removed from the town's small commerce square, this ridge offered long-range views of one of the largest rivers in the state winding through the mountains. This captivating view, of course, meant the walk to and from the town was (and still is) long and difficult. Surprising, or not, the city chose this location to build the city's public housing community. Spread down the mountain, poor families continue to move in and out of the cheap housing available.

For many years in her county, my grandmother fulfilled requests for white and black dolls. Her biggest clientele were white farmers' wives, and she told me once that the white women of her town requested black dolls more commonly than they requested white dolls. She thought it odd, but I figured that Grandma was the only woman making black dolls. Farmers' wives could pick up a white doll at any store or arts and crafts show, but the black dolls felt rare in their all-white social circles. Grandma didn't sell any dolls to black women, she said, but not because she was prejudiced. She explained that she talked to some black women at the grocery store, and occasionally in a restaurant, but these women had no way of knowing she was a doll-maker. I wondered what the black women in town noticed or knew about my grandma. She knew so very little about them, keeping a distance, perhaps, because racialized assumptions made black folks seem deviant. In the grocery she probably interacted with black women who wore heals, dresses, and pins in their hair as often as they wore work boots and blue jeans, just like she did. How could she make sense of the black stereotypes that contradicted her lived experiences?

Much like Jemima and Sambo, Grandma's black dolls served as symbols of southern pride and relics for nostalgia. The images of

Jemima (the plump, happy cook with her hair hidden inside a red kerchief) and Sambo (the eager, young boy with torn pants, a bare chest, and a big sense of humor) worked together to convince Southern whites that slave times were somehow gay for us all. These were stories with which I disagreed. Though I wanted these dolls to signify Grandma's critical consciousness or progressivism, though I wanted to pay attention only to her stitches and craftsmanship, I knew that these black dolls lived out racialized existences sitting on freshly made beds or clean shelves in white folks' kitchens. No one talked about racism or slavery or prejudice. And, no one apologized for celebrating and normalizing racial stereotypes. We all just carried on, believing that things were okay and that intentions mattered more than outcome.

I went to college believing that ignoring race was the most progressive, inclusive thing I could do as a concerned white person ideologically opposed to racism. My parents thought that talking about the race of a person was rude, so they taught me to whisper descriptions of race as a gesture showing *lack* of racial prejudice. I never asked why race was named only when storytelling about people of color.

When I started graduate school, my family was not prepared for the many conversations I would re-remember from our collective past, and the questions concerning race that I would come home to ask. I often experimented on my family, devising strategies for talking in an everyday, casual way about embodied racial prejudice. I created conflict by posing ideological questions, and then I tried to transform the difficult dialogues into productive, transformative moments. I practiced and practiced, but my attempts usually led to explosions and mutual frustrations. Deep riffs between my sister and I emerged during the 2008 election when she sent me an email naming Obama as a Muslim. Since when did being Muslim pose a threat to American nationalism? And didn't she know that Obama was Christian? I didn't know how to respond to the email, but I wanted to understand what she intended. Between tears, I relayed the story during a graduate school seminar and, later, had to report to them that my sister was "just joking."

I heard during my childhood that *our people* were too poor to own slaves. This was the case on both sides of my family. My dad's family were sharecroppers, and my mother's were landowners, but neither, apparently, had the capital to own others. Even as a child, I found this rhetoric repulsive. It implied that they *wanted* to own slaves, but couldn't for economic reasons. I wondered if humanitarian reasons factored in at all? I wished, I hoped.

During a trip back home in 2008 to conduct research for my doctoral dissertation, Grandma's black dolls resurfaced. My parents had agreed to watch my four-year-old son while I conducted oral history interviews with white southerners about the rhetoric of racial identity. I was in search of answers about what makes a white person racially "progressive?" How does one act out a "progressive" white identity? And, what words work best to interrupt racism?

Two airplane rides, a two-hour car trip, and the loss of three hours time coming west to east, airport home to airport home, left my son and I groggy and irritable. I placed my sleeping boy on my parent's double bed, and pulled the antique quilt back, unearthing one of the black dolls. Memories materialized as I brushed my hand over the knotted hair and the crisp apron. In the darkness, I debated about what I should do. If I left the doll on the bed, my son would surely see it. He might find it odd that Nanny had only one black doll on her bed when she didn't have other dolls out on display. I knew the other dolls—black and white—were tucked away in the massive trunk placed at the end of her bed. I wondered if she selected a black doll as evidence of her progressiveness. Most people in my family claimed colorblindness as their way of interacting with the world. If everyone could just stop seeing race, then racism would disappear. If Mom picked a doll at random, and it happened to be a black doll, how could she not notice race once she placed it on the white quilt? I wondered if she contemplated on this choice at all. Perhaps she just saw Grandma's hard work and became reminiscent about her mother, who was shrinking with rheumatoid arthritis an hour away on the farm. I felt guilty for holding the doll and for pondering so long about what to do with this moment. I wanted clarity. What move would prove the most critical and strategic one in teaching my son about white privilege? In a desperate attempt to protect my mother from her own lack of intention, and to protect my son from my own ignorance, I rushed from my parent's bedroom and stuffed the black doll into a closet just as I had done twenty years earlier.

Things They Carry 83

At breakfast the next morning, I asked my mother if she remembered my first sleepover with a black girl. She made quick eye contact; her body changed shape a bit, and I could see she was frustrated that I brought up the subject.

"Why, yes," she said, her gaze intentional, warning me not to press forward.

I grabbed a blue and white plate, purchased decades ago with S & H Green Stamps, and scooped eggs for my son and me. My mother rarely sat with us during visits, and she never ate breakfast with us. She just busied herself around us, cleaning countertops, washing dishes, making lists, or folding laundry.

"I remember," I started again, "that first time Jones came over. I was careful to hide all the black dolls in the closet. I worried they would make her feel uncomfortable."

My mother looked over her shoulder so that I could see her face, but she didn't say a thing. She gestured toward my son, indicating that our conversation was over.

Hiding the dolls in the closet was pointless, then and now, because I neglected to hide all the other racial paraphernalia that populated our house. When my friend Jones spent the night, she went into the bathroom and saw my mother's *Little Black Sambo* book stacked on top of *Ten Little Indians*. Jones came out of the bathroom carrying the two books, both featuring drawings of children in captivity. Perhaps she hadn't noticed the ceramic black figure sitting on my mother's bathroom sink. He wore tattered red pants that cut off just below the knees. His black chest and feet were exposed, and his head was bald. His lips were unrealistically red against a very white beard.

Other than the one black doll, I thought my mother's collections of black stereotypes had been tucked away, here and there, since the year I started high school. My son had not been exposed to the tea towels cross-stitched with black caricatures. He had not seen the many ceramic salt and pepper shakers shaped like Jemima and Sambo; their black faces broken in half by wide red lips. And yet, the same books sat on the back of my mother's toilet as resided there twenty years ago. Behind the clear glass in the dining room, I found a few of the salt and pepper shakers, once I looked for them. These collections demonstrated just what kind of white people we were, and this was not an image I wanted to share

Things They Carry 84

with my son. Though, it wasn't a history I suddenly decided I didn't want to hide either.

"Do you still have the book about little black Sambo?"

My son asked, "Who's that?"

I waited for my mother to fill the silence. I wanted to hear her explain the book, though I knew she couldn't. This book was a memory in her childhood, the same as jam cake and the smell of my grandfather's pipe. Her aunt sent this book, written in 1899 by Helen Bannerman, in the mail when Mom was less than seven years old. It sat out in her room until she packed it in a box and took it to college for one semester. Then she got married, dropped out, and the book ended up on display in the bathroom. I read it many times while going to the toilet. In the story, four hungry tigers cornered a young boy from India because they wanted his umbrella and fancy blue pants. Sambo's face was so black that only the whites of his eyes were illustrated, even though "Sambo" usually refers to someone of multiple races. After the young boy gave the tigers all they demanded, vanity churned the tigers into butter, which Sambo's mother used to make pancakes.

"It's a book that Nanny has from when she was a little girl," I explained to my son. I considered whether I should show it to him this visit, or if I should wait until he was older. I didn't want to exoticize, trivialize, or confuse. "The book has important lessons in it." My mother glared at me disapprovingly, and turned quick to walk out of the kitchen.

Part of me wanted to assemble my mother's collections in front of my son. I wanted to line them up, black shoulder to black shoulder, and listen again for the stories they might tell, the memories they might stir, and the histories I had overlooked. Just because I had not drawn my son's attention to the figures that were tucked around mom's house did not mean they had gone unnoticed. By not talking about them, I normalized such representations. I made it easier for my son to think in stereotypes about other racial groups.

"So," I began, "Sambo was this little boy who lived in South India who was trapped by tigers and they began harassing him, just as white colonists would do. He outwitted the tigers, though, by appealing to their vanity . . ."

LETTING GO OF HISTORY
by Cristina S. Mendez

My history teacher once told me that the American Revolution and Declaration of Independence were so radical because they represented a new perspective, a new idea and ideal of what "revolution" meant.

What did he mean by saying that? (Keep in mind this same history teacher had drilled into the minds of malleable young people that wars were fought for the wealthy and by the poor.) I assumed this was another drilling—a reinforcement—of those same ideas.

I was wrong.

My history teacher explained that these actions, these words, were meant to symbolize a new idea that revolutions were okay, that they were sometimes necessary and justified. Many of us, if we are "good" Americans, at least have read these words, written in blood and ink by our great founding fathers:

> "Governments are instituted among men, deriving their just powers from the consent of the governed; that, whenever any form of government becomes destructive of these ends, it is the right of the people to alter or to abolish it, and to institute a new government..."

Simple words. Powerful words. Banned Words.

Would you dare to speak these words in front of the White House, or the Pentagon, or any government building for that matter? Would you dare make a case to show the "destructive ends," of our government and demand to institute a new one? I dare not. Because these words aren't okay to say anymore—unless, of course, you are talking about the "Glorious History" of the Greatest Country in the World.

Which reminds me, reading these words for the first time, written in wisdom and righteousness, I felt empowered. Yes, this government was constructed for the people and by the people. But have we, as a people today, listened to our founding father's advice? Have we, as a people, exercised our rights "to alter or to abolish" the government or the laws created to subjugate us against our will?

Is it time for a revolution?

It could not possibly be—this is the Greatest Country in the World, right? But we all know that certain current events made my words cause your breath to pick up a little. Or maybe they didn't. I wouldn't know. Don't let me be the wiser—I'm young and ignorant with radical ideas about revolution—and there is that **banned** word again.

Radical. Revolutionary. History.

So let us consider, and perhaps admit, that we forgot, or didn't pay attention to, or neglected our country's history. The great proverb says that history repeats itself. History teachers use this as a tool to get us interested in history. *Recognize the patterns. Learn from them.* History teachers try to help us to understand the past—the good, the bad, the ugly. But we don't, do we? At least not all of us do. *We*—as the American people, as a self-elected government, as a united nation—may see the atrocities, the "destructive ends," but we ignore them, or brush them off, or turn away.

What does it matter if we do turn away? Who will it affect exactly? Take a foreign war for example, and as the U.S. is currently involved in eight, I'll let you take your pick. Like any other war, censorship reigns over the masses. Most of the real atrocities are cleansed by the media, only allowing a portion of the real "destructive ends" to make the nightly news.

Take a second to think—do these wars affect us? In the sense of everyday life, maybe the answer is no. We will probably go to work tomorrow morning and come home in the evening and everything will be the same. But think about it mentally, economically, politically—think about it in terms of the future, in terms of children and grandchildren—would these "destructive ends," though far from home, be enough to put the Declaration of Independence into motion? Would it empower you to demand a new government?

For me, the answer is simply yes. For me, it is time for a revolution—that horribly despicable, unpatriotic tabooed word. Yes, *We* need it desperately. Maybe not governmentally, or politically or economically—but socially. (And maybe those areas need some work too. Let us not get too *radical*, however, for we may be silenced, hushed, closeted.)

But consider society as it is:

It is not wrong for a fourteen year old to be having sex, smoking weed, binge drinking, starving themselves or committing suicide. It is not wrong for *our* culture to include, and accept, mass shootings and drug abuse, poverty and crime. It is not wrong for a country to be at war with eight different countries, subjugating the people to social, political and economic enslavement and exploitation. It is not wrong for war veterans to be on the streets, struggling to survive. It is not wrong for families to starve in a first-world country. It is not wrong for three-year-olds to be prescribed Ritalin because they may or may not be a little hyper. It is not wrong for the bravest of us, our Great Soldiers to pose beside the mutilated bodies of children.

No.

None of this is wrong.

Come on now, don't be so Radical.

RAGS IS RICHES
by Charles Tarlton

In order to stand well in the eyes of the community, it is necessary to come up to a certain, somewhat indefinite, conventional standard of wealth.
—Thorstein Veblen

The premise is simple: those super-large bundles of blankets, tarps, sleeping bags, rugs, grocery bags stuffed with old clothing, tablecloths, towels, old rags, boxes, plastic bottles and watering cans, piled inconceivably high and precariously onto grocery carts and mobile dumpsters along the Embarcadero, in San Francisco—are, among the homeless, the basis of invidious or envious comparison. Wealth, even for them, is the determiner of social status.

On the pier, where you can watch the Alcatraz tour boats go out and come back, there is usually a row of overloaded grocery carts, piled high with junk. You have to look carefully to discern which ragged, bearded, and stocking-capped indigent belonged to which cart. But when *the messenger*, a small old woman dressed militarily, hops between carts, the proper owners look up and acknowledge his or her own chattel.

The messenger's purpose is to tally the cart's inventory, and to communicate the verdict to the panel of judges sprawled along the row of benches on the other side of the flower beds. They decide who is the wealthiest, not forever and all time, but just for the day—today's *chief man* of means.

Without this ritual, there would be very little reason for them to live, as far as these vagrants are concerned. They had either missed or foregone the normal pleasures of love, comfort, and a well-fed feeling. Some, for reasons beyond their control, lacked a snapped synapse in the brain or had an overdose on rubbing alcohol, while others had wandered morally into lives of crime and dissolution only to wake up one day with all the doors slammed in their faces.

Each day was a new ordeal; the body cried out for necessary nourishment, which was not easy to come by. Often, they fed on garbage, or the odd handful of change pressed into their hands by a guilt-ridden retired professor or slumming matron. But, even in these straits, there was energy left over for each to worry about their position of standing relative to the others. Words were measured carefully before being delivered, if only because it was well-known that they would be carefully weighed at the receiving end. Rank and relative status were all that remained of ordinary life.

Against this background, is Bill Ogilvy's story. It starts when he has just a boy in Oklahoma. He came from a *normal* home, with *normal* parents, in a *normal* town. At the age of fifteen he was arrested for breaking into a 7-11, and did a stint in juvie before hitting the road.

At each significant juncture that followed, Bill somehow chose wrong and continued on a downward path. Finally, while in an Arizona prison camp he was beaten almost to death by a bored guard, and received permanent and significant brain damage. When he was released, years later, he drifted and drifted—(*to move or pass passively or aimlessly; to be carried involuntarily or without effort in some course or into some condition,* OED)—until he ended up in San Francisco, vaguely hanging out with a gang of similarly damaged people along the Embarcadero.

As you might imagine, this new life was at first without purpose or meaning. Bill moved through each minute as if through mirrors, stunned by the incomprehensible duplication on all sides. When he spoke, he heard his own voice as an echo; the voices of others were a roar, a chatter, and a boom! Several times he was picked up by EMTs and taken to the hospital where we has pronounced beyond help, only to be returned to his fungal existence.

One day Bill happened to be sitting near the pier where an accumulated-wealth-contest was in progress. He was busy counting on his fingers, and trying to attach significance to anything at all, when the little messenger came up to him by mistake. She mistook assets belonging to the Monster—that was his handle, this loud, crazy, giant of a man who always wore a gray overcoat and had white hair down to his shoulders—piled very high on a four-wheeled utility cart, for Bill's. (Bill at this point had no possessions). Once the mistake had been corrected the Monster actually befriended Bill, and began his education into the accumulation of wealth.

Bill was proficient to a fault, literally, as he had no real idea of what he was doing, and would just see and take, as he bounced through each day. Monster taught him to hold on to his stuff, to work an oversize grocery cart from Walmart into his consciousness, and to derive pleasure from the growth of his pile.

In time, Bill often found himself the winner of the little conspicuous consumption contests, largely because it was now the only thing in his head. He grew to be resented among the other contestants. They said that his single-minded devotion to the gathering of stuff was the product of a mental deficiency and ought not to be allowed, or at the least, there should be some sort of handicap that he would have to work under. But no two of them could agree, fearing that a rule for one might easily spread to become a rule for all.

One night, on a day when Bill had won seventeen property contests in a row, and the little messenger had pronounced him the *winningest* contestant ever, he was attacked. He wasn't hurt, but his possessions were untied and unpacked in a frenzy and tossed along the waterfront (some actually into the Bay).

Bill must've known it was beyond hope, his precious accumulation lost forever. He sat down on the pier, leaned back against the wooden railing, and started to cry. The crying became uncontrollable sobbing and wailing, and in an overflow of emotion, a discharge of energy that had been repressed for several decades, Bill stood up and took a swing at the first person he saw.

It turned out to be a security guard that worked at the Alcatraz ticket booth. He easily subdued Bill, who went back to sobbing, and then, out of necessity (one we can easily understand) he called the police. They came and took Bill away.

Most of us waited a long time, expecting Bill to come back. After several weeks, the flow of events filled in over Bill's removal, and the surface of life among the invidious comparers was smooth again.

⇒ *COMPASSION CITY*

CLOSE TO MY HEART
by Gail Jeidy

These are the memories I carry.

Picture me, a forty-year-old new mother again, cuddling my newborn on the sofa. It's four o'clock in the morning, the TV's playing in the background while I breastfeed Mattie, named after my grandmother. Eleven years later, *Mattie*, now "Jamie," a name she thought suited her better, comes home from school and wants to talk about bras.

"The girls at school wear pastels."

"What girls?" I ask, wondering how my *little girl* became so concerned with bras.

"They all do."

Did they even sell pastels in the girls' section, or were her friends *already* shopping in women's?

We go to the mall. I head straight to the girls area, when she stops me.

"Women's, Mom." Her tone is innocent, not pushy.

"I think these are more for you, dear." I point to the girls' display. "Pretty, aren't they?"

"Can we just look?" She pleads with the same raised eyebrows I had at her age.

In my tweens, I was shy. I didn't talk to my mother about *intimate apparel*. We talked about whether to set juice glasses on the table for dinner or what dessert I'd prefer, apple crisp or chocolate pudding—not girl stuff.

Jamie leads me through the colorful aisles of women's bras. She zigzags clear of the ultra-sexy, push-up models and pauses to deliberate a G-rated rounder. She knows what she wants, makes her selections, and retreats to the nearby dressing room. I sit in the overstuffed chair outside the door to wait. Moments later, she comes out, her heart-print T-shirt, stylishly layered over a tank top, reflects in the mirror. She's shy too.

"How does this look?" She twirls and looks at me with doe-like eyes, all pupils.

"Which one is that?" I can't see the bra she's modeling, but can tell it's lightly padded.

"The pink one," she says.

Hmm, hard to judge. "Nice," I say.

She returns to the dressing room for the next round.

How I wanted a bra at her age. All the girls had one. At night, I studied the tutorial on how to determine my brassiere size in the Sears & Robeck catalog. I calculated my chest and cup size using the yellow tape measure from Mom's sewing basket, and then took my assessment uptown to J.C. Penney's where I loitered in the lingerie department. I was the girl in horn-rim glasses strolling head-down past the 38-DD racks, peering up in a blinding blizzard of all white bras in hopes of finding 32A. Okay, 32AA.

In my day, we called it *Junior High*, not middle school. Seventh grade was the worst. That was the year we started taking required showers after gym class; it didn't matter that we hardly ever worked up a sweat.

On the first day of gym class, I join the cloister of girls around the locker room benches, until Miss B strides in, announcing, "Okay, girls, suit up." We get busy changing, exposing our white underpants and bras, under identical navy gym suits, our last names printed in yellow block letters on the back. In the gymnasium, we do warm-ups and play dodge ball. Afterwards, we retreat to the locker, where there's a definite lull before Miss B waltzes in. "Well, what are you waiting for, girls?"

And just like that, we nod and strip.

The soft mounds of tissue, masquerading as my breasts, hustle to the showers right behind my best friend, Darby, who had true breasts—two rounded cups with a prominent dark circle and distinct, pink, protruding nipples at the epicenter. Darby doesn't hide. I can't help peek out of the corner of my eye. Hands turn and knobs twist, and water and words and squeals spurts forth; one girl, in my peripheral vision, skirts off behind the private curtain.

The showers go quick. Back at the bench, time slows. I try not to look around the locker room at the shapes and sizes and degrees of what my mother calls *development*, and especially not at Betsy Baboola, the girl with the biggest breasts sitting at the end of my bench. I dress quickly, my plaid jumper zipped and hanging on my formless stick of a body. Betsy dries herself off slowly and gently, as if she's toweling a baby. She dresses just as slow, letting her huge breasts hang while she clothes the lower half of her body first. She steps into her underpants, then her miniskirt. Next, she fastens her bra before pulling on her frilly white blouse and buttoning it up the front. She takes longer to get dressed than anyone else.

The dressing room door opens and Jamie reappears, the bra beneath her shirt bulges unnaturally.
"What do you think?" I ask, trying to be supportive.
She twirls, straightens up and studies herself in the mirror. "It doesn't feel right."
Too much padding, I want to say before she disappears behind the door again.
Moments later, she's back at the mirror, with an *I'm pretty* head-toss. "What do you think of this one? It's lavender."
I nod my approval.
Back and forth with a new bra, twirling again in her heart shirt. "Pale yellow," she says.
She's comfortable in her poses and unaware I'm watching.
Light blue. Turquoise. Peach. "Two more," she says, smiling.
Jamie carries her two-bra selection—a lavender and a pink—to the check-out counter. The next day, she leaves for school feeling good.

I wanted big, full breasts like Betsy Baboola. I admitted this to no one, not my mother, nor my brother, Mark, who used to hang from the attic door to elongate his back, in hopes of growing six-feet tall like the instructions promised in the mail-order kit he bought.
At night, I lock myself in the bathroom and inspect my growth prospects. First, I notice a bit of change in my right breast, then the left one a month later. Any day, I expect to see Betsy Baboola breasts reflecting back at me because that's what happens when a woman *develops*. The months pass, my brother continues to try to stretch his spine and I keep watch at my mirror. Years pass. There's change, but never the big change I'm expecting. Bottom line: I pale in comparison to the standard set by Betsy Baboola. (But Mark, fully grown, reaches five-foot-nine and a half.)
I turn seventeen. I have a *sweet* boyfriend who gives me his football jersey, number twenty-two. A week later, on pep rally day,

Things They Carry 94

I wear it to school, passing him and his friends in the hall. They laugh and elbow one another. "Is that her chest size?" I'm devastated. He blames one of his friends and says, "You're fine the way you are." I hear the words, but don't believe him. Three days later, I forgive him. We go out for five years, get engaged, break up and never see one another again. He gets married. I get married. I get divorced. He gets divorced.

Sixteen years later, we reconnect and eventually get married and have two beautiful children, including Jamie, who turns seventeen, and wants to be *Mattie* again. She's slim, beautiful and well-endowed, and *loves* shopping at Victoria Secret.

I can't precisely remember when I quit caring about breast size, but I've been comfortable with my size throughout adulthood. Still there came a time I felt bustier than Betsy Baboola— during my daughter's 4 a.m. feeding. Her heavy lids fluttered and closed, and I sunk into the sofa and watched Shirley Temple in *Baby takes a Bow*.

I'm making new memories now.

I carry the pink purse I bought at the retro shop three months before I got the news. It spoke to me. It was a nice contrast to the reoccurring gray skies.

I carry the memory of the private waiting room where the doctor performed my biopsy. There was a box of tissues on the table and a framed inspirational message of hope on the wall.

I carry the emotion of the night before I heard the results, in the hotel room, when I leaned over to my husband and whispered, "I'm scared."

I carry the memory of standing in Disneyland with my pink purse, and my new orange and pink shoes, and getting the call. What I heard was, "You have breast cancer."

I carry the memory of Sally, the kind messenger, delivering negative news, but couching it positively.

I carry the memory of my two daughters mirroring my emotion as I lower my head and collapse in tears. And me feeling that I'd ruined their spring break.

I carry the memory of my husband Ron by my side throughout everything.

I carry the memory of my first meeting with the surgeon. She discussed the planned mastectomy and reconstruction options.

"Some women skip reconstruction," she said. "And some even get tattoos. There are lots of choices."

Twice during the exam, she referred to my breasts as *small*. My ears perked up, causing me to chuckle inside, thankful to no longer be seventeen.

Mostly, I'm carrying thankfulness for a good prognosis and for burdens that are lighter because I'm not carrying them alone.

⇒ *FICTION*

I WASN'T THERE
by John Poblocki

I needed the money for an engagement ring for Jackie, my high school sweetheart. After all, it was the height of the Viet Nam War and there was a pale of resignation that life had to be lived right then and there, or perhaps not at all. I had witnessed too many lives left unlived, so when Lloyd asked if I was interested in working overnight at the shoe factory, down by the river, stripping and waxing the office floors, I had to say yes. It's a decision that I have carried with me to this day.

I didn't know Lloyd except through my part-time job pumping gas at the corner Sunoco station where he was a mechanic. I worked there during vacations from college, and we had very little in common. He was a high school dropout who was drafted into the Army, and did thirteen months in the jungles of Nam, returning home to a career of greasing car chassis.

If you went to college you got an automatic draft deferment as long as you carried enough credits to be a fulltime student and didn't flunk out. I was in my senior year waiting for one of three things to keep me out of the war: a draft deferred job offer (there were plenty of those if you knew where to look); a 4-F physical draft deferment (which my doctor had virtually promised for a football knee injury); or worse case, a slot in the National Guard. Anyway, I wasn't going to Viet Nam. I was going to finish college and then marry Jackie as soon as she returned from her senior exchange year in Paris; and I couldn't let her leave at the end of the summer without a ring on her finger. Besides the easy-outs, I was opposed to the war, which by 1968 had become very unpopular. I was never one to go against the flow of public opinion, so that may also have been a factor. And let's be right up front: I was scared shitless of taking my last trip in a body bag—aka, a coward's deferment.

Lloyd and I had barely spoken in the summer of '68 even though we worked together almost every day. When Christmas break came that December, we picked up where we left off, pretty much ignoring each other, until he needed help with an overnight job stripping floors at the Hudson Shoe Factory. I was reading a book in the gas station office when Lloyd walked in stirring his coffee with his screwdriver.

"Hey, college boy, how would you like to make fifty bucks for one night's work?"

"I'm game. What do I have to do, drive the getaway car?"

In 1968, minimum wage was around $1.30, so fifty bucks was almost a week's pay for someone like me pumping gas. Lloyd didn't get my joke or chose to ignore it. He always looked like he was about to go off, which made me a little uncomfortable. I think I was afraid of him even though he and I were about the same size. There was just something about him that was intimidating. Something unpredictable. I knew I could match wits with him intellectually (maybe surpass him a little), but he had thirteen months of experience killing people he didn't see eye-to-eye with, or maybe didn't have fond feelings for. Either way, I didn't want to piss him off.

"The job is easy if you're not too much of a pussy college boy who needs his mamma to tuck him into bed by ten. I'm used to going thirty-six hours on patrols in snake and tiger infested jungles, and then sleeping in a swamp with leeches sucking my blood. Working all night waxing floors is like a vacation for me. For you, it's probably too tough. I'll just find someone else, *pussy boy*."

"What are you saying? Just because I go to college you think you have the right to disrespect me."

"Yes, I do, Pete. It gives me the right. Just because I *didn't* go to college, doesn't give you the right to ignore me all the time." A moment passed. "I'm giving you a chance to make some money, not be my friend. You want it or not."

"I want it." A moment passed. "I don't mean to ignore you. It's just that, that…"

"Forget it."

Next day, we both worked until seven, me pumping gas and washing windshields, while Lloyd replaced a clutch on a '56 Buick. His normal appearance was a little unkempt. I don't think Lloyd had washed his hands, face or hair, or by the downwind odor, any other body parts in a few weeks. His pickup truck had a similar ambiance. Lloyd drove and I sat on the broken springs that served as the passenger seat. I could watch the street through the open floor.

On the way to the shoe factory, we picked up some beer, burgers and fries and drove down to the base of a steep, mostly dirt driveway, past a nonchalant security guard in a shack. The sprawling red brick, four-story mill complex had large, old windows (a few had been broken by kids throwing rocks), a flat roof and a loading dock that sat between two sections of the plant. The river ran along the other side of the mill opposite the parking lot. It was dark with minimal outdoor lighting. Other than the security guard, no one was around at the factory.

He parked his rusted hulk near the loading dock under a floodlight, I took out the food and beer. Lloyd reached into the greasy fries with his dirty hands, then licked his fingers and grabbed another handful. I decided against the fries and stuck with a burger and beer. We ate furiously without talking. Afterwards, Lloyd ran up to the office to unlock it, while I lugged the stripping machine and buffer, along with drums of stripping fluid and wax, out of the back of his truck.

By the time we got the equipment and supplies to the second floor, he downed three more beers. Said it was the lunch he didn't have time for. I wondered how this night was going to turn out.

We started by moving furniture from one office to the next. I was in charge of logistics and muscle power. Lloyd provided moral support. When the first room was empty, we began pouring stripping fluid on the floor; Lloyd said he was real good at pouring stuff and laughed. I didn't get it, but by then, he was up to six beers.

While I ran the stripper across the linoleum, Lloyd sat and watched. I didn't care much because it was easy work, and he was drunk enough to worry me.

Suddenly, he jumped up and said, "Hey, pussy, can I show you something? I only show my *friends*."

"So we're friends now?"

"Sure we are, Petey boy." He tried to entice me. "Bet you never seen this kind of thing before."

"All right, I'm game."

Lloyd stumbled his way out to his truck, and came back with a little bag made of what looked like Chinese silk, with a drawstring at the top. He leaned into my face, shouting, spraying me with his beer spit. "Know what I got in here? Know what's in my little bag of tricks? Huh, college boy?"

"Whatever it is, it can't be legal."

Lloyd was about six-foot three and a hundred and seventy pounds. He was wiry and had a wild, aggravated, fearless look. It got more fearless as he got drunker and made me nervous. He opened the bag and accidentally spilled the contents on the floor near the stripping fluid. It looked like dead mice or parts from some dead, dried up animal.

"God damn it! Pick my ears up! Don't let them get wet from that shit."

The contents looked a lot like little ears: dried dark brown and black and all shriveled up. I thought it was a Halloween prop, like something from a joke shop, and reached down to pick them up, when a hairy thing fell out of the bag; I caught it in my right hand. It was also brown and black and all scabby. I suddenly realized what this stuff was.

Lloyd had dropped on the floor, rolling back and forth holding his knees, and screaming with laughter. He rolled into the scrubber and knocked it into me. I was freaking out, figuring they had to come from Viet Nam. I pictured someone lying in a rice paddy, gasping for their last breath, and seeing buck-toothed Lloyd laughing at them, right before he cut the ears off.

A few weeks before, the press carried stories about the My Lai massacre, where hundreds of civilians were killed by US troops. I had wondered who could commit such atrocities; not what *kind* of person, but *who*, actually, *the person*—and here he was.

Lloyd saw I was repulsed, making him laugh even harder. He eventually stopped and picked up the ears and scalp. I went back stripping the floor, but after the initial shock wore off, I wanted to talk.

"Lloyd, how did you get that stuff?"

"You mean my trophies?" Grinning, Lloyd said, "Shit man, I can get some for you too. I sent some back home to my old man and he thought it was funny. My platoon did this shit all the time. If you saw what we saw, you would've got some souvenirs too. It was how we got along. We actually had cuttin' contests. We cut off other stuff too."

I put up my hands to stop him there, a sick feeling washing over me.

Things They Carry 100

He kept talking. I wanted to ask him *why*, but was afraid to, since he seemed to be sobering up. He took a step towards me, looked right into my eyes; I thought I could see something in him at the verge, like he was about to breakdown. Instead he said, "There was nothing wrong with it. *Everybody* did it. You don't get it, college boy. These *gooks* were killing my friends. And I got even by taking their ears. Sometimes I took their eyes too. Those bastards deserved it."

I finally said, "Isn't this wrong, Lloyd? I hope they were dead when you started cutting them up."

By Lloyd's expression, I could tell the thought had never occurred to him, like it was a revelation that killing someone and cutting them up, not necessarily in that order, was not okay. He looked deranged, and screamed into my face through a spray of spit with his arms flailing to the sides. "Fuck you. You weren't there. You were sucking your mother's tits when I was living in a fucking jungle. I saw my best friend half eaten by a tiger. You didn't see what I did. You didn't sleep in a swamp with snakes for six months. So shut the fuck up, mother fucker." Blue veins extruded in his neck and on his forehead.

I thought now was a good time to get back to work stripping the other half of the brown linoleum. Lloyd looked like he wanted to kill me, but actually started drying the floor. He worked like an insane person, banging and throwing things that disagreed with his effort, all the while mumbling more curses under his breath.

The job was nearly finished around four in the morning. I had already put the furniture back in place, and Lloyd had brought the equipment back to the pickup. I headed to the loading dock, and found Lloyd sitting at the edge of the platform with his feet dangling back and forth in a rapid, exaggerated, forced cadence, not in a relaxed way, but like he was winding up to explode.

I said, "Job's done, Lloyd, why don't we go get some breakfast. It'll be time to get back to the gas station for the morning shift soon." I wanted to leave. I didn't really want to be *alone* with this guy down by the river behind a shoe factory at four in the morning.

He met my eye, the light giving his face a monster-like shadow mask. He seemed drunk again, but when he spoke, I could tell he was completely sober. He said, very deliberately, "Pete, my friend, you don't know shit. You weren't there. You can't judge any of us. Unless you saw your friend blown up right in front of your eyes, the same friend who said he'd be point-man on patrol when it was really your turn. You can't be my judge and jury. You and the rest of your hippy dippy ass friends against the war who don't know shit." Then he started to sob with his face in his hands. He cried hard, his body heaving uncontrollably. "No one asked him to run point for me. He just volunteered. Maybe he just wanted to die." A moment passed. "None of it's my fault, man. Not the ears and shit. What the fuck do you think I am, crazy?"

He went on, "Don't you think I know it was wrong? They were stone cold when we found them. Dead and rotting. Don't you think I have nightmares every single fucking night about it? Every time I hear a noise I jump or duck for cover 'cause I think it's an incoming. I see the point-man on every street corner. I hear him calling me. I hear babies crying all the time, and when I look around, there's no one there. Where are the babies crying from, their graves? I'm losing it, man. I can't take it anymore."

"Lloyd, is there someone you can talk to? Maybe the Army has someone to get you through some of it?"

"The Army? No way am I going to talk to those crazy motherfuckers. No way!"

I didn't know what else to say. I wanted to help, I really did, but I was so tired, I could hardly focus my eyes. "We can talk more tomorrow," I offered. "Let's go home and get some sleep."

Lloyd started the truck, the engine sputtered and the tailpipe spewed blue smoke, as we drove up the ramp out of the Hudson Shoes parking lot.

By the time he dropped me off at my house, it was five-thirty. "See you in a couple of hours?"

He gave me a dead stare. I wanted to tell him it would be all right, but went in, tucking the fifty bucks in a safe place until one day I saved enough to buy the engagement ring.

After a few hours sleep, I got to work at nine. Lloyd should have too, but he was MIA all Saturday morning. He never even answered his telephone.

When I closed up around two, I drove out to Lloyd's place with the owner of the gas station. Lloyd lived in a rented, run down dump of a trailer five miles up the river, near the falls. His truck had been parked in the backyard; his German shepherd, leashed, paced back and forth along the river, barking.

We went to the door and knocked. When he didn't answer, we banged louder and shouted for him, as if to wake him. It was now going on three; he should've been up by now, even after working all night.

That night, after we called the police to report Lloyd missing, they found his body in the river, about a mile downstream, caught on a submerged branch not far from the Hudson Shoe Factory. Where I accused him of doing bad things. Where I looked into his soul and then let him go.

Later that night, the police asked me what Lloyd's frame of mind had been before he dropped me off. They were unsure if it was a suicide or an accident.

I wanted to tell them I had pushed Lloyd too far, but only said, "He seemed fine."

"There's nothing you can tell us?"

"If you want to know the truth," I started, but didn't finish. I thought about Lloyd, and the other two or three million soldiers that were sent over, who were still living with what they'd seen. How many others ended up just like Lloyd?

"Well?"

I walked home trying not to think about whether I was the reason Lloyd had jumped into the river, or if he had thought about it before he even met me. Only Lloyd had the answer.

What I did know—and what I'd learned from Lloyd—was to never question another Viet Nam vet about what they *did* or what they may've seen.

I had no right. I wasn't there.

AND I'LL BLOW YOUR HOUSE DOWN
by Susan Levi Wallach

That be us, walking down Pringle Street, a container of gasoline heavy between us, our hands crampy against the damp plastic. Jerome in his blue Love Shack t-shirt and me with bare chest, both smiling under a low, bare sun that feel like warm honey. We filled it halfway at the Cheap-O. "You boys run out of gas again?" say Eddie, already jumped-up from the stuff he sniff between customers. "Yeah, but we getting lots now," I say. "That why we doubled up." He laugh like anything, like it the funniest thing he could hear.

The container hold fourteen gallons, which is why Jerome figure he need my help. I tell him seven are enough, though I don't know for what and he don't let on. You can do something with seven gallons. "You got matches?" Jerome say, casual-like. Like we just talking, on our way nowhere. Like we still in grade school: "Want a smoke? Got matches?" Jerome always the one itchy to light up.

"Third time you ask," I say. "Still same answer." Pat the bulge of my pants pocket. The box of strike-anywheres make a sound like pick-up sticks collapsing. "Got enough," I say. Lift it when Eddie wasn't looking, when he throw back his head, laughing at his own not-funny joke. Teach him to laugh like that, when Mr. Jack takes inventory and Eddie can't account for a box of matches.

We walking to Alma's house down a morning street that shimmies with August heat and smells of pig grease and eggshells. We cross the railway bridge out of town, past houses with chicken-wire fences that sag into the sandy ground and stumpy trees that strain for the sky. Jerome start to whistle. "This is going to be a good day," he say. Then he snicker and bump the can against me with his hip, like we going to bust into a dance, him whistling the accompaniment. Like Alma ready to open herself to him again.

Alma live on Lemon Tree. From Pringle me and Jerome turn onto Paradise, then onto Swan. Lemon Tree is gravel and hardpack and wild tamarind, more path than street. It wind along the track behind the Goodwill store and the Price-a-Penny, where nothing priced a penny but most things cost under a dollar and have hot-pink tags that read 28¢! 53¢! 36¢! That exclamation point throw a lot of people, who take it as a guarantee that they getting a deal.

Things They Carry 104

They don't bother to figure out that a roll of toilet paper at 53¢! cost more than a dozen rolls for $6 minus the punctuation.

The guy who owns the Price-a-Penny drive a blue XJ6 that he have to park on the downhill side of the street. "You see?" he say. "You buy here, you save enough money to get yourself something special."

He sweet on Alma, or so she say. Grab her last night when him closing up and she the last customer at the checkout counter. Grab her and stick his tongue in her mouth, swirling it around like she an old mason jar with honey at the bottom. Hmm, hmm, he moaned, his tongue whipping the ridges of her palate. Or so she say in her bee-nectar voice when Jerome phone her. Which peeve Jerome no end. Alma think she know how to play him.

"She tell me all that, no saying what she not tell me," he say. He reach over and pull my ear to make sure I get his point.

I shrug away from him. When he toss the gas container through my kitchen window that morning, I run out the back door and hide in the shed. Jerome sashay himself up the driveway. "Toly? Where you at? You somewhere here, I know it. We got a job."

I figure he mean fetching gas for someone who visiting one of his neighbors and find himself stranded after Jerome drain the tank clean and already sell what he get at half-price to someone else. But Jerome's breath smell of mackerel, no sweet hint of sucked petroleum. So I can't figure it. It's too soon for Mr. John to want another fire in his pizza shop, the first two hard enough to set up, what with new-employee Jerome twice poking pinholes into the gas pipe behind the ovens.

But Alma.

At the corner we rest the container on the curb and Jerome take a stolen box of Milk Duds from his pocket. He stuff a fistful into my mouth, then offer me some. His eyes daring me to spit. I swallow one at a time. They go down like bruises.

"That Jerome is some sot," my mam once say, even with Jerome right in the house. She mean it in the old sense: a fool, because Jerome don't drink even water.

"Aw, mam," I say, to make it sound like a joke, so that Jerome don't take it in his head to rub his fingers along the shelf where my mam keeps her ebony-glass figurines—82¢! at the Price-a-Penny, scorpions and wasps with stingers thin as snowflakes—so he can accidentally brush a few to the floor and step on each one.

Sometimes Jerome lose his balance. Hard enough for him to see through his one eye, the other a milky marble since I made me that slingshot. I walk into the schoolyard and yell, "Hey, Jerome." As he look up, I fire a pebble right toward his belly. But it hit his right eye. In Jerome's flat world, his hand always closing on air. Every morning he wait for me to pour his coffee and light his one cigarette for the day.

We walk slower now, Jerome busy thinking up his action plan. When we pass through the gate in front of Alma's house, Jerome suddenly let go of the handle he holding, and my shoulder stretches from its socket. Then he sit on the gasoline container, while I go knock on Alma's door.

The curtains bunch at the windows—none of this overheating air get into that house. It is cinderblock and brick, but the door rattle under my knocking. I imagine myself a big bad wolf, huffing and puffing and sending that door soaring over piggy heads. When Eddie owned the house, the door had an iron grate over it, but Alma take it down the afternoon she moved in.

Alma come to the door with her hair corkscrewed around bits of rag, her bathrobe pulled tight at the waist, her palms piggy-pink. She squint at me, and I turn my head toward Jerome, so she understand the problem.

Jerome stay perched on the container like it some toadstool and he some mouth-blown glass spider. His shirt is the same grease-streaked red as the container. Alma look at him. "Ay-yi-yi-yi," she say, her voice expressionless. Alma read minds for a living. Whatever she see now in Jerome's don't worry her. If anything, she look bored. A man with fire between his legs. She run across this before. Maybe she knew we coming. Maybe she know how it turn out. She come out onto the porch to where the tamarind shade it.

"Why he bring you?" she ask me.

"For courage," I answer, though what I think about is the weight of the gasoline and Jerome's flat world.

"Nah," she say. "He bring you so you stop him." She snort. "So far, it look like you fail." I turn toward Jerome, only to hear the door slap against the frame and the lock click into place.

"Hey," Jerome yell. "You supposed to get her out here." He still sitting on the container, but I have sense of unseen movement, of his muscles winding underneath him.

Things They Carry 106

"We should go," I say. From inside the house come heavy wailing music and the sound of a toilet flushing. Maybe Alma has company. I put my ear against the door but it is only Alma's voice I hear, assaying near-keyless high notes.

Jerome glare at me, not mean or anything. Just expectant. Wanting me to bang the door again. Or kick it, because even a bare foot could make that wood give way. Let Alma know that some serious shit could go down in her yard. But I don't. Everyone say that Alma throw spells, that she spun Jerome's head her way with a chant over a pot of sweet onions or cookies baked with mistletoe and vervain. It turn him docile, till that docility make him nervous and aggrieved.

"Alma," I call. "A-a-l-m-a-a. . . ." I feel my pocket. The matches jiggle like change. I picture Alma on the other side of the door, pulling the rags from her hair. She open the door in her working clothes: a patchwork dress and white sandals, hair in a halo, on each long finger a silver ring. In her hand she swirl a shot glass of grainy rice, from which she swear she divine patterns and truth.

"You two have to leave," she say. "I got someone coming." But she say it like an invitation, her eyes right on Jerome. Surely, she work some new Jerome spell while getting dressed.

Jerome slap himself on his thighs and get up. That thigh-slapping thing is how Jerome signal he mean business, the way a gorilla pound his chest. He take a step toward Alma, but she fast, putting up her hand right away to stop his traffic. For a few minutes, we stand around waiting for one of us to decide what to do.

I'm hoping Jerome forgot the container and what he intended it for, but by now the smell of gas is all over, its own flower stronger than the pots of jasmine that Alma grow to hide what the wind carry from the garbage dump. Stronger even than Alma, whose legs enclose a flower more pungent than any Crimson Glory rose in my mam's garden.

I move my eyes to the container, slow so not to startle Jerome. There's no sign of a leak. I decide it's Alma's doing, her way of letting me know to get going. I wonder what juju she's preparing to send my way. A swarm of gnats hover around my face, and I swat them away, sure they are Alma.

Things They Carry 107

"Go get yourself some water," Alma say. Jerome shake his head, but his eyes on her, so I sidle over to the hose. I check my pocket again.

"You wet your hair, they won't bother you," Alma whisper as I pass her.

To make sure the rubber taste in the water is good and gone, I let it run onto the tamarind till the soil bubbles. Then I take my time lapping at the spray, feeling it soak into my shirt, giving Jerome and Alma a chance to lock eyes so that Alma can spread herself through him. Neither one pay any attention to me. I stay till the matchbox make my pocket sag. When I straighten up, Alma give me a smile.

"Give up, Alma," he say, his lips slick with meanness. She say nothing.

"Give up," he say again.

Alma still say the same nothing.

In the silence, Jerome nod at me and walk slow to the street. He amble down Lemon Tree, so I can catch up before he get to Pringle. From the porch, Alma stare at me, her face dark as ebony glass. I know what Jerome expect me to do. Open the container and tip it to the ground. Let the gasoline spread till the dirt bubble into bits of iridescent shell. Flick a match against the cement. Leap through the gate while a great whoosh of flames eat up Alma's jasmine, porch, house. While Alma scream her ay-yi-yi-yi and pull at her hair.

ROOTS OF GREEN
by Rachel Routier

Can you tell me one thing you identify yourself with?

Black. The one color I understand. Black, the color of the night sky, mirrors my hair, sparkled with gray like the stars. Black is the label of my skin. Black is the meaning of my name. Black clothes shroud my withered body since my husband's demise. It was an obsidian-tipped spear that pierced his side, while his blood pooled black on the earth, the strong scent telling me his life was leaving burnt my nostrils. He used to tell me he fell into my eyes, two dark basins, and that he never wished to escape.

Black is the sole color I've ever known, for I am blind, you see.

You come to me here in India, a traveler, lost and wandering the world. Your purpose in life is unknown. You bring with you fancy equipment and questions. The others tell me your cameras hold images and memories inside them to tell later. You tell me the year is 1998, but what does that mean to me? You, traveler, seek to learn my secrets. And in these secrets, you shall find yourself.

Your tribe has gone through so much. Will you tell me more about the tribe and its practices?

My tribe is old, ancient like the trees we worship. We have lived in the humid lands of India for many centuries. The trees gift us with life. Their boughs canvas our paths, bear the fruits we eat, and house the animals we stalk. Our name, *Ki Hynñiew trep,* means "the seven huts." The largest blessing is the bridges we create together, tree and human. And this is the secret you seek from me. Is it not why you've come?

When I was a young girl, still learning the dark world differently than other children, my grandfather took me by the hand, and said, "It is time to learn the ancient art of your ancestors."

"But Daadaa, how can I in the dark?" I asked, my other hand flailed in the open air, bracelets jangling.

"Your eyes hold the beauty of the world," he told me. "Now you will take the world and show it your beauty."

My five-year-old mind failed this logic. I missed my friends. We had just begun wearing a suki, the soft garment girls draped about their bodies. My younger brother, Jordi, ran wild with the other naked children in the village. But I was the eldest of the family, and tradition called for the eldest to carry on the ways of our people, regardless of whether the child was a boy or girl.

"Devoki, pay attention close now, child." Daadaa took my hand and placed a slim root on my palm. My tiny fingers curled around the root no larger than my pinky.

"With this root, you will build a life-force that will last five hundred years. Your children's children will use them. They will feel your presence in the interlacings. You will be with them forever to support and protect their family. Devoki." He leaned closer; I felt his breath on my cheek. "You are going to become a bridge weaver."

Can you tell us more about the process of building the bridges?

The bridge lessons continued through many years of my life. It would take many years into the future to learn the skills I have by my age.

Daadaa explained, "Long ago, our ancestors noticed the powerful roots of the fig trees. These trees perched on boulders and hung their roots where they pleased, even across a river. Normal trees would not work for bridges in our home. The wood would rot from the rains and moisture in the air.

"Listen closely now, Devoki, the bridges are made through the generations, and with each generation, the bridges grow stronger. The first generation plants a fig tree. They tend and watch the sapling throughout its younger years. As the sapling grows, the second generation coaxes the roots across the river using hollowed-out betel nut trunks that have been sliced down the middle. This creates a root guidance system and support for the fig tree. The third generation constructs the bridge when the roots are strong enough to support a person. Each generation must tend and care for the existing bridges while strengthening and growing new. The tree bridges allow us to cross the rivers without having to travel for long distances in search of a safe place to cross. The trees cradle us and keep us safe. Eventually, the trees' roots will drape across the river, while the trees stand tall and proud."

When I was still a young girl, Daadaa took me to three locations near the river, where I planted the fig tree seeds that would, with my help, come together to form a bridge over it. Each tree would bear long roots and branches with glossy leaves wider than the palm of a man's hand. I grew with the trees, and over time, Daadaa taught me how to guide the roots of the trees to join over the river. He also showed me how to tether the betel nut trunks from one side of the river to the other for the tree roots to grow through.

How we did it took time and patience. We coaxed the roots to grow straight across the river and into the banks of the other side, where another tree grew. We intertwined the two trees' roots and I felt them grow strong. He guided my hands until I needed guiding no more. Together we cared and guarded the trees from any harms or threats, be it man-made or weather.

Eventually, my grandfather's breaths became labored, and then the paths grew too difficult for his weathered body. His trees grew high above him, and stood proud and tall when he could no longer.

When he died, Jordi and I buried him beneath a Boroi tree. The waxy leaves shaded the dirt that concealed his body. I covered his grave in a variety of flowers. I smelled each one to make sure Daadaa would like them. Jordi said they were all beautiful.

Your grandfather sounds like a great man. Will you tell me more about him?

My grandfather possessed the patience of the trees I coaxed into growth. I'd often fall into frustrations by the complicated patterns for the betel nut suspension tethers I could only touch and not see. When I'd reach these points, he would take me to the bridges of our ancestors.

Here, he described to me the scene I could not see alone.

My grandfather told me how the sky shone. It hung like a wide blue belt amongst the vibrant life of the jungle. The wide leaves of the trees did not grow long enough to stretch across the mountain river. Water torrented below the bridges and down waterfalls and crashed on boulders. I could hear its roar. The people were safe, however, from the hunger of the river because of the tree bridges. Bridges, as wide as a three-year old child is tall, grew across the furious waters and breached a nine-meter gap, at its narrowest, and provided my people with a way to cross the falls. With braided

Things They Carry

roots cultivated from the Bayan tree, the ancestors made handrails. Then they connected smaller roots from the handrail to the bottom of the bamboo plank for further protection. Wide, smooth rock slabs, held in place by the roots for hundreds of years, made a pathway for travelers' bare feet. The bridges were alive and growing, a brilliant green, Daadaa told me, which I imagined to be something full of life, vibrant like the laughter of children.

Besides giving passage across the falls, the bridges provided a way to trade and commute with other villages that lay beyond. Otherwise, we would have no way to reach them. The falls crash down the entire mountain. They never relax. They slam against rocks with a fierce anger, an anger that has claimed the lives of those who try to tempt the falls.

And your husband, Hari, what happened to him? I have record of a raid that occurred here, how did that come about?

Hari and I have known each other since I was thirteen. He became my husband and guide to the seeing world, and we brought four children into the world. We spent many years together. As for my brother, Jordi married a village girl and his children grew alongside my own. They played together and ran throughout the village like we once did. My eldest became my protégée. I guided her hands along the roots and taught her how to coax growth from the trees. I held her face in my hands and told her the same story my grandfather told me. She was the next generation.

Over time, I listened to the sounds of my children's laughter till it grew to the deeper tones of adulthood. My hands became rough and calloused, twisted from years of use. Though they never tired from holding my grandbabies.

You asked about the raid, so I will tell you.

The sounds of the jungle changed with the seasons, but one year, the trees rattled with the sound of war. The air became hot and dry. Our lips cracked. Food fell scarce. The murmurs of anxious tribesmen caused the birds and babies to quiet.

Some of the tribal leaders said, "Other tribes are raiding villages. Fifty-three years of peace broken." Others cried that there was no food, and sought the gods to explain the strange drought that year in the wettest land on the earth. "We must pray to the rain maker," the people cried.

Our bellies shriveled to nothingness. Babes cried for food that would never come. Many of them succumbed, along with the elders. Hari and I managed to survive. Death was not yet ready to claim us, but it *did* claim one of my grandchildren. All the children of my tribe were like my own children, so we mourned together in silence, as is the way of my people. We held each other close and swayed together like the sound of the boughs of a tree moving in the wind. The rustle of our clothing and tree leaves blurred into one sound.

When the news arrived of the destruction of our neighboring tribe, Hari called our eldest son and his eldest son and they began to sharpen the spears.

The sound of stone-on-stone grated my ears and I cringed with every stroke.

Can you tell us a bit about your husband, Hari?

Hari. He was my sight.

I tended the trees alone for many years after Daadaa died. The bubbles of the stream and roar of the falls became my conversation. Each stone knew the feel of my foot. The roots rippled at my touch. One day, when my childhood was behind me, and I had stepped into womanhood, a shadow blocked the heat of the sun from the spot where I lay next to the mountain stream.

My body tensed to run.

"Hey, Devoki, it's Hari." The shadow said.

I relaxed. Hari had been frequenting my growing bridges as of late. I felt him settle next to me on the fallen palm fronds. His hand slipped into mine.

"Devoki." His hushed voice floated close. "The constellations are almost aligned. My parents say it could be any day now. They watch every night for the lucky stars to shine. Then we can be wed."

Since my parents died long ago, Jordi had been making the arrangements of my dowry, even though he was two years younger than me. I imagined in my mind his proud, lanky frame stood tall up to Hari's father's shoulder while they negotiated.

"Tell me again what the stars look like," I said and leaned back against his shoulder.

What happened that night? Can you tell me more about it?

The night the bridges burned? Yes. I was with Jordi and Hari's body on the outskirts of the village, where they left Hari to fall and die alone. They being a tribe a few villages over, who had never bothered us before the drought. They snuck up on Hari while he was on watch. This tribe became fierce with hunger and destroyed other villages in their starving rage. Ours fell next. They started the fires. They killed Hari.

That night Jordi took me to Hari's body, a fierce scream dropped us to our bellies in the midst of my mourning. I laid my head on Hari's arm. It was still warm. Jordi cursed under his breath, but I held a finger over his lips to keep him quiet.

Seconds trickled.

Jordi shifted and turned towards me. "They are burning the bridges."

"Why?" I asked.

"They took all the food," he said. "They don't want us to follow across the rushing river."

I sunk deeper to the ground. The beautiful bridges my grandfather devoted his life to—*I* devoted my life to, and my daughter devoted her life to, were dying. The hiss of the green roots' life screeched into the air. The sounds of weeping and yelling, mixed with war cries, fell silent to the sounds of our ancestor's work falling to the flames.

The ancestors mourned in silence, from behind the veil.

I left Hari's body and stumbled a few feet to the bridge paths I knew well. I stopped short when the heat hit my face. Jordi followed and stood next to me.

My wails filled the air first. They unlocked the silence of the others, and soon, the villagers came out one by one to surround me, to witness the green roots' death. I screamed for the trees, for Hari, and for myself.

I'm sorry to hear about Hari. What exactly happened the night of the raid to him, if you don't mind me asking?

That night, I woke to screams of women and crying babies. Outside my hut, our warriors roared the war call of our tribe, and fought the enemy back. The blackness held a feeling of terror; I tasted it on my tongue. I gripped the edge of the grass sleeping-mat I shared with my husband. But he wasn't there when I reached out for him.

"Hari?" My voice croaked. I tried again.

A snap of a twig and I swung my head towards the sound.

"Hari?" My voice stumbled through the darkness.

"It's Jordi. They have taken over the entire village. I've taken the children and mothers into the jungle to hide. Come on, I'll take you to them." His steps moved closer to me.

"Where's Hari?" Stubborn to the core, I refused to be moved until I had an answer. I could smell smoke in the air.

Jordi answered me with silence. I could feel his lean frame radiating tension.

"Jordi, tell me right now. Where's Hari?" My old voice shrilled and cracked. I grabbed his arm. My hand slipped off. His arm was slick with something wet.

He took a deep breath. "It was his watch to keep guard. They got him from behind with a spear. He didn't have time to get away. All the young men were exhausted and he insisted it was good use for an old man. I'm sorry, Devoki."

I sat straight and still, and placed both my hands flat on the mat, the braided pleats dug into my palms. I pulled them up. One stuck to the mat from the sticky wetness from Jordi's arm.

"Take me to him."

"It's a war out there. You don't understand. You can't see." I could hear the disbelief in his voice.

I broke. "I need to feel him. I need to touch my husband's face one last time."

Jordi took my hand and held it to his face. It was canyoned in wrinkles much like my own. I could feel it wet with tears. "Please don't do this."

"I have to," I said.

He nodded his head and took my arm. His palms were slicked with sweat. "If I say run, run."

"Yes," I whispered.

We ducked out of the hut and crept along the outskirts of the village. I could smell the burning homes and hear the crackle of the flames. A few villagers wept in hushed tones. I counted the steps we took. Fifty. One hundred and fifteen. Three hundred and two. With each step, I held my breath till the next one.

Things They Carry 115

On the four hundred and seventeenth step, Jordi stopped. He didn't say a word. But he took my hand and guided it until it touched the face I'd known since I was thirteen. Hari's face was slack. The wrinkles of his skin drooped. His eyelashes brushed my fingers. I closed his eyes. His lips were cracked and open. I ran my fingers through his hair; my hand came back wet; the bottom of my suki was also soaked with his life-blood.

"His blood is black," I said. I found the spear still in his side. I could tell from the cold smoothness of the flat front and sharpness of the sides, it was obsidian.

"How do you know?" Jordi said.

"Because I see it," I said.

Now, traveler, you have heard my secrets and listened to my story. The village thrives and flourishes once more. My heart still hurts, but my family helps to keep it whole. My daughter planted new fig trees with her oldest son watching. She nourishes and cares for each one like I taught her, and like my grandfather taught me. Your fancy cameras and equipment hold no value here. We have our minds and bridges. But the machines have whirled and clicked regardless. Maybe now the cameras hold your purpose. Tell me, traveler, what do you see?

A HISTORY OF ART
by Jennifer Falkner

Italy, 1768

    The inn may have been the largest in Trieste, and convenient from the port where Winckelmann booked passage to Rome, but it was not the grandest place he had ever visited. The gold medallions he carried from Vienna, awarded to him by Empress Maria Theresa, weighed heavily in his pocket, reminding him of his importance. While he waited for his luggage to be brought up, he surveyed the faded brocade curtains, the shabby cushions on the chairs by the hearth, and the framed paintings on the walls—desultory depictions of ships he could easily see regularly at the harbor. He sighed. It was after all only temporary. A place to rest before the final leg of his journey.

    Once settled in, and the gold medallions hidden away, he searched for a distraction. He searched for a boy to liven things up. In the square, not far from the inn, he found the perfect one loitering beside the fountain, not up to much of anything. His profile caught Winckelmann's eye, and when the boy turned, his sublime countenance took his breath away. Though the late-afternoon sun which broke from behind the campanile temporarily dazzled Winckelmann, it couldn't keep him from recognizing the sensual lips, the dark expressive eyes, that perfect nose. It was Antinous—the young *beloved* of the Emperor Hadrian, once reproduced in marble throughout the Roman Empire, the most famous boy in the world—come to life. Winckelmann approached.

    His name was Francesco Archangeli. An unemployed waiter. "Ah," said Winckelmann, a trifle pedantically, "You're in between restaurants."

    "You have a job for me?" His accent was rough, uneducated.

    "A job? No. Perhaps a position. As my companion. Just for a few days." Winckelmann's voice trailed off. The June sun was bright, causing him to squint at the fountain. "Would you accompany me to dinner?"

    He knew how it looked, a middle-aged man with a forehead that seemed to be racing to the top of his head, with the perpetual slouch of a scholar, walking back to the inn with a bright, beautiful boy twenty years younger. It was the Seehausen Latin School all over again, where he, as the newly-appointed assistant headmaster, made a fool of himself over a student. At the time, he shared a room with the fair-haired Wilhelm Lamprecht, and frightened the boy with his passion. He remembered sitting across from him at a candlelit table. Lamprecht's hand spread flat across the book they worked from to hold it open; Winckelmann had been too afraid to touch his pale skin. Instead he tutored him in Latin grammar, chanting declensions like they were declarations until they were closer than brothers. It was a friendship without equal since the ancient world. He dubbed them *Orestes and Pylades*.

And then disaster.

Everything should have started with a kiss, but a kiss was what ended it. The kiss was only a shade more than fraternal, and dangerous in a country where perversion was a capital offence; it terrified Lamprecht. What followed were visits from Lamprecht's father, then a magistrate, and then an admonitory meeting with the headmaster. Ugly words and angry letters came next. Lamprecht went home, and Winckelmann, broken-hearted, moved to smaller lodgings.

Later that evening, Francesco lay along the foot of the bed, turning over Empress Maria Theresa's medals in his long fingers. Winckelmann told him how the palace in Vienna, where he had received them, had glittered, omitting how he had gotten thoroughly drunk. Even after years of being a celebrated writer and an authority on Greek sculpture, Winckelmann was still uncomfortable at these sorts of events. He vaguely remembered the Empress holding his thin hands in her bejewelled ones as if they were old friends. She had called him a hopeless romantic.

Francesco's fingernails framing the medallions were encrusted with dirt. Winckelmann looked away. He didn't want to be reminded of Francesco's lowly origins. The remains of their dinner—pork rissole—littered the table beneath the room's only window.

"I write books, you know. About sculpture. Art. I'm really quite famous." Winckelmann didn't know why he felt the need to impress the young man. Francesco's services were contracted for the duration of his stay in Trieste. But something impelled him to go on, as if their relationship would continue after he left.

"Are you rich?"

Things They Carry 118

"I don't even own my own house."

Francesco studied his tailored coat, its glittering buttons. "You have rich things."

"A weakness of mine. I love beauty. I confess, a dream of mine is to own an antique statue. Not a Greek one. Not an original at any rate. Not even anything very big. A Roman copy would do. But I could never afford it."

The young man allowed Winckelmann to stroke his cheek with the back of his fingers, to loosen his shirt, even pull it from his breeches. In his excitement, Winckelmann couldn't stop talking. He described some of his favorite sculptures. Names like Plato and Polykleitos floated into the evening air. Gradually, he whispered the names of body parts as he uncovered them, reverently, with the precision of an anatomist.

Afterwards, when the only sounds in the room were from the braying donkeys outside and a dog barking in the distance, Francesco slept. His legs were spread wide apart, the sheets pushed down around his ankles. His lips were parted slightly and a vague frown pulled his eyebrows together. He was perfect. Winckelmann understood the urge to capture life in marble. He gazed at his very own Barberini Faun until sleep pulled his own eyes closed.

Winckelmann awoke alone. Listening to the traffic below the open window, he stretched into the empty space beside him. Thoughts of his first journey to Rome filled him. He had been running away then too. Leaving his parents' home in Prussia as a student had been a revelation. He'd travelled through Florence and Naples, where artefacts and discoveries excavated from Herculaneum were carted in daily.

One afternoon while in Naples, he saw three statues that had been unearthed beneath the floor of a theatre, what had once been a wheat field. The museum hadn't even catalogued them, and they changed everything for Winckelmann. The marble draperies that the Greek women wore were frozen in a permanent flutter, like fine linen in an invisible breeze. Their hair, carefully executed in a style that resembled wedges of melon, was overshadowed by the nobility in their features, their elegance and air of quiet meditation. In short, they were *divine* to him, enough so that he couldn't get them out of his head. What made them beautiful? What made them superior to everything that came afterwards?

As if possessed, Winckelmann wrote an essay exploring the answers in a night and a day. He scribbled relentlessly, not noticing the cramped room he had rented, the noise in the street, the peculiar smell of rotting fish that wafted through the open window at dawn. He sent it to Rome, where it was published quickly, and soon, he found his name celebrated by artists and philosophers. It was his emphasis on the *essential*, the element that the Greeks sought to perfect, that became so popular. The refined simplicity of Greek sculpture went beyond mere elegance, it was ennobling.

But ideal beauty, he wrote, *could not be detached from life. It reflected the culture of the ancients that produced it. Therefore—the only way for us to become great, or even inimitable, if possible, is to imitate the Greeks.*

Winckelmann preferred not to remember the other notable event from that time, when Rome showed him for the first time the true delights of the Greeks. After publication, he quickly moved in exalted circles, and became friends with painters and sculptors and minor royalty. In order to fit the role of *aesthete*, he affected turbans and fur-lined robes, and kept his new apartment in Rome in wonderful disarray. And then came his more than passing acquaintance with Casanova, which led to usually delightful and unexpected visits.

Except once.

Casanova had knocked and entered Winckelmann's rooms without pausing for an invitation. Perhaps he heard some noise, some wordless grunt that he took for a German greeting. Winckelmann imagined Casanova describing the scene later to a mirthful audience at a dinner party in Trastevere. His seeing Winckelmann, out of breath and with rosy cheeks, hastily pushed the serving boy—he had one in every city—away, his voice trembling as he dismissed the lad.

Casanova, amused, reclined on the sedan and apologized for interrupting.

Winckelmann strove for an attitude of cool sophistication.

"As you know, I'm researching the ancients. I decided to enlighten myself through practice." *You old fraud,* he thought to himself, *you Catholic pederast. Casanova is laughing at you. Soon it will be all over Rome. Where is that heavenly delight now? The Greek purity?*

Casanova grinned.

Things They Carry 120

Winckelmann saw rows of even white teeth. Winckelmann's own teeth were discolored, preventing him from giving more than a closed lip smile. He hated him. His perfect teeth, his dark puddle-like eyes which lovers found so intoxicating. The physique was nothing much, no Praxiteles had been at work there. But when Casanova finally—finally—left, Winckelmann noticed his narrow hips and rounded buttocks beneath velvet breeches. Ripe apricots on a bough were less delectable. The door closed and he groaned. He wondered if the serving boy was still hanging around the kitchen.

On the second night in Trieste, Winckelmann dressed up for his paid guest. Instead of his traveling clothes of the previous day, he donned a white linen blouse with gold buttons inlaid with carnelian and one of his favorite purchases in Rome, a pair of black leather trousers. Perhaps he thought his attire would in some way make up for his own lack of personal beauty.

Francesco arrived late, but brought food from a stall outside. It was warm and oozing. He licked Winckelmann's fingers clean; Winckelmann thought he might faint. Francesco had raised his eyebrows at the leather trousers and said nothing. He seemed to have undergone his own transformation during their day apart. His lips seemed thinner, less sensual, his eyes blacker. He must have been to a barber, for his dark curls had been tamed, slicked back so that Winckelmann could see the little rows made by the comb's teeth.

They ate, saying little, then Francesco matter-of-factly began to undress, beginning with his shoes.

"My father was a cobbler," said Winckelmann. "If I had learned, I could have mended these for you." He picked up the shoes one by one and ran his fingers along the thin leather uppers, poking them through the holes in each heel.

"You could buy me a new pair." There was something fierce, challenging in Francesco's voice Winckelmann did not like. He forced himself to laugh.

"I could. Of course I could. We'll do it tomorrow," he said. "What does your father do?"

"Drinks, mostly."

"Do you have brothers and sisters?" Winckelmann thought of the half-timbered house in Stendhal that he grew up in, the narrow front room that served as dining room, parlor and workshop, with cobbler's tools hanging from the wall. Perhaps he should have gone all the way home instead of turning back in Vienna.

"Why all the questions? I thought I was here for a fuck, not a catechism!"

Francesco's fury was disquieting. It stiffened every muscle. Winckelmann was reminded of a *kouros*, the body perfect in detail, but the face a frightening blank. He did the only thing he could think of. Reaching for the boy, he dropped to his knees.

There were good years. Years when he barely thought of his family in Prussia. He had settled in the Villa Albani, on the outskirts of Rome, cataloguing the collection of Cardinal Albani, chief librarian to the Vatican. He wrote a series of *Reflections* on Greek art and culture that brought him a degree of fame, as well as more scholarly works on antiquities. In all his writings Winckelmann argued that the Greeks recognized the younger male, often adolescent and even slightly androgynous, as the perfection of Beauty.

His friend Anton Mengs advised him to give it up. "It's no good, you know, making friends with these young men. Trying to educate them about beauty and philosophy. They never understand what you mean and you invariably get crushed."

Winckelmann didn't listen. He wasn't made for the coenobitic life. By then he was already cultivating a new disciple, Baron Friedrich Rheinhold von Berg. His new beloved embodied his every ideal. Twenty-six, educated and moneyed, a young nobleman ripe for a finishing education. They used to picnic in Frascati, discussing philosophy and art. He created reading lists for the younger man, Homer, Plato's *Phaedrus*. He quoted Cowley to him:

> I Thee, both as a man and woman prize;
> For a perfect Love implies
> Love in all Capacities.

And he carved Berg's name into the bark of a sycamore. Convinced theirs was one of those special friendships that few mortals were blessed with, Winckelmann compared them to Achilles and Patroclus, Alexander and Hephaestion.

It didn't last. It never lasts and Berg eventually left Rome for livelier Paris. Winckelmann had been a slave to Berg's form, its eurhythmic proportions. He missed watching the muscles beneath Berg's skin ripple across his back like water. When he described the marble fragment of a statue of Hercules, for another book on sculpture, it was the memory of Berg that inflamed his prose. Winckelmann compared his grief with that of a mother mourning her child. He may love beauty but beauty, he was learning, did not always return that love.

The third night in Trieste something was wrong. Francesco's eyes were too wide, blank and staring. He moved too slowly, and held his mouth in a stiff, small smile that pushed his cheeks back into a semblance of a child's rounded face. He was not beautiful at all. When he spoke, words rattled out too quickly, like a hail of stones on a roof, and Winckelmann had to pause to render them into something comprehensible.

"This is the last night, signor. You pay me before you go like you promised, yes? You pay me tonight. In gold."

Winckelmann was distressed by this change. Was this the effect of opium or some other drug? He wished he knew. Could coffee reduce its effects like it could for drunkenness? But he didn't have any coffee and dared not leave Francesco in this state while he fetched a cup. He could induce vomiting, but somehow knew Francesco wouldn't let him close enough to try. Sleep. That was by far the best cure. Francesco could sleep it off and perhaps there would still be time for a proper goodbye in the morning.

Casually, using his charms, he brought Francesco over to the bed and encouraged him to lie down, not noticing the crafty expression that passed over Francesco's features as he complied. He removed the waiter's shoes and pulled the thin sheet up over him. He trailed his thumb down the side of Francesco's cheek. Why hadn't he ever noticed these pockmarks before? And the lines around his eyes? Francesco seemed to have aged a decade in two days. Winckelmann moved over to the window where lights danced on the water in the harbor. Somewhere among those hulking dark ships was the *Calypso*, ready to take him to Rome in the morning. His friends, his books, his work was waiting for him. The thought should have made his heart feel light.

The sun slipped lower, burnishing the lapping water. Winckelmann pulled the Empress's medals from his pocket and turned them over in his hands, letting the light play over the regal profiles.

There was movement, a footstep, behind him. Then something fell around his neck. A thin cord, tightening even as he tried to peel it away. Winckelmann threw his elbow backwards, hitting his attacker solidly in the ribs. The tension in the rope slackened, Winckelmann jumped up and twirled around. Francesco—his angel, his faun—confronted him with a knife in his hand.

"What are you doing?" He wondered if Francesco would understand him, his dilated pupils looked emptied of thought. Francesco raised the knife.

Winckelmann saw it arcing through the air, like a chisel, on its way to his heart. He panicked.

Oh God, help me!

The knife came down, but not in his chest, like he thought. Much lower.

He screamed. Francesco dropped the knife. As Winckelmann continued to scream and voices collected outside, Francesco looked around, something like awareness flooding into his face. He snatched the medals that had tumbled to the floor and bolted.

Winckelmann fell to his knees, clutching his groin, now a handful of gore. Pain squeezed the air from his chest. The world turned black, it swam with strange voices. He wanted to tell them, to explain.

He was only a scholar. A lover of art.

RECOVERED MEMORIES
by John Mueter

I.

London, 1821
38 Great Poulteney Street

    The long-awaited report of my journey to the continent has been sent off to the publisher and will appear shortly, after I am no longer to be counted amongst the living. It has been arranged. In the account the public will read I felt compelled to censor and conceal the truth about certain matters. The world is not yet ready to receive the full, unadulterated account of my intimate life with his lordship. And so I have taken it upon myself to provide here a candid history describing that memorable summer on the shores of Lake Geneva in the year 1816.

    Five years have passed since those unfortunate events transpired at the Villa Diodati. It is early afternoon on a warm August day as I put ink to paper at my desk for the last time. The thin curtains flutter silently by the open window. When I have finished writing this version—the unadulterated account—I will secrete it away in a locked drawer in this desk. Perhaps it will see the light of day in the distant future, a time I can hardly imagine. Perhaps then, in a more enlightened age than this one, the pain I have experienced will be acknowledged and understood. Loving the wrong person made of me Misfortune's Child. The object of my love, my devotion, was the poet George Gordon Noel—Lord Byron.

II.

April-May, 1816
London to Geneva

    Few people can claim one incident in their lives that changed everything forever, that propelled the trajectory of their existence into an entirely different orbit. I, John William Polidori, remember the day, the very hour, when my life was altered utterly. I had just completed my studies at the University of Edinburgh and had received a degree as doctor of medicine the previous year. I believe that, at nineteen years of age, I was the youngest person ever to do so. Being most eager to establish myself as a practicing physician, I moved to London in the early spring. My mentor, Dr. Halford, had taken an interest in my budding career and introduced me to Lord Byron. His lordship had been looking for a personal physician, and Dr. Halford thought I would be most suitable for the position. The good doctor had no idea how this meeting would dramatically change my life.

We were invited to tea on that April afternoon. Upon entering the elegant salon I espied a covey of women fluttering around a man of aristocratic bearing. It had to be him. Eventually we approached the party and I was introduced to his lordship. Those first impressions have etched themselves in my memory. It was not merely a matter of his personal appearance (though that was certainly of merit), but that he radiated a vigor that was strangely compelling. He was an enchanter, a magician, one who drew people to him like moths to a flame. I subsequently got to observe that unique quality during the few months I was in Lord Byron's company. It still remains a mystery to me.

While I was being formally introduced, I noticed how Byron sized me up. His powers of perception seemed to bore through me, his ample brain must've made a thousand calculations as to my character and my general suitability to his purposes. Later we had a private meeting. He enquired about my studies and my medical experience. I shared with him the salient points from my thesis on somnambulism, a subject which was of particular interest to him. He asked if I was proficient in mixing potions. I knew exactly what he meant. It was no secret that the upper classes, and especially artists, indulged in the pleasures of laudanum, a derivative of opium. I assured him that, as a physician, I had access to every kind of medicinal substance and was adept at concocting anything he could desire. A slight smile appeared on his fleshy lips at the mention of the word. His gaze lingered on me a moment too long and betrayed an interest in me that was more than just civil. I had an inkling then that he might *desire* more than mere opiates.

How can one describe a personage as famous as Lord Byron? There are many written descriptions of him as well as a number of portraits. He looks curiously different in each one of them. The man was a chameleon. He was of moderate height, with thick, curly dark hair. At the time of our first meeting he was reasonably proportioned. Later on, his weight had a tendency to fluctuate greatly. One of my duties, after I was officially hired on, was to monitor his food intake and advise him as to proper diet. It was a losing battle. Byron was a man of extremes, of unbridled passions—but more on that later.

He was one of those individuals who could look entirely different depending on the circumstances: how he was turned, the angle of the light, the time of day. The very emotions that preoccupied him would dramatically affect his visage. There were times when I thought, *Now there is a handsome man!* Other times I thought he was less so, but always interesting to look at. He possessed superior strength in his upper body and was a proficient swimmer—a few years prior to my appointment, he had famously swum from Asia to Europe across the Hellespont. Sometime later he would swim the entire length of the Grand Canal in Venice.

These are no mean feats, to be sure, but one cannot avoid mentioning his infirmity, something about which he was extremely sensitive. He was born with a malformed right foot, a clubfoot. He endured various attempts to remedy the situation, but they only caused him pain, and did nothing to help in the end. He refused to wear a brace. Instead, he learned to cope with his limp and mask it. The power of his personality was so strong that I am sure many people who met him were not even aware of anything amiss with his physical person.

I was only twenty when I came into his lordship's service. I was young and impressionable. Byron was already famous and infamous at the same time. Everyone in Europe knew about his literary accomplishments and his scandalous exploits. The gossip circulated about him like brisk autumnal winds.

Despite his immense fame, Byron was hounded out of England. He had a bitter separation from his second wife just at the time I met him. The woman was angry and had been spreading horrible, spiteful rumors about his treatment of her. For all I know they may have been true. But of one rumor I am sure, Byron had relations with his half-sister Augusta, and that the child she had bourn the previous year was his. He admitted as much to me in a moment of intimacy and trust, in the days when such existed between us. Rumors of this illicit, incestuous affair flew about England. One can hardly imagine the scandal it caused in society!

My own background was decidedly ordinary. The circumstances I grew up in were a far cry from the world of wealth and privilege that Lord Byron enjoyed. My Italian father, a man with some literary accomplishment to his name, met and then married my English mother in London. She was a governess at the time. The family moved to Scotland when I was still a child. I think Byron was pleased to have a Scotsman as his personal physician and traveling companion. He himself was a Scot, but as a member of the aristocracy he rooted out every vestige of the Gaelic from his speech. I never heard a trace of it pass his lips, except in jest.

Having inherited my father's swarthy Mediterranean looks, I frequently heard it said that I was handsome. It was not such an asset when I was growing up, however. At Ampleforth, the school I attended, I was mercilessly taunted for looking different and for having a foreign name. I learned that being different was not a good thing. On reaching adulthood everything reversed itself. It was Byron who first made me realize that my looks were something desirable. He liked women, there was no doubt about that, but he also had a weakness for men of a certain sort. His taste ran to small, youthful men. I seemed to fit the bill. Although I was not short (actually an inch taller than he was), because of my delicate build he perceived me as being boyish. He even made me shave off my dark chest hairs at one point. I didn't mind. Whereas he pursued anyone who wore a skirt, he was very particular about men. During the time I was with him I never saw him pursuing another male, certainly not in the way he pursued females. Women were potential conquests to him; men fulfilled another need entirely. For a while, I was the one who fulfilled that need.

III.

Four days after I met Lord Byron we were on our way to the continent. Everything Byron did was dramatic, unusual, eccentric. He had an enormous Napoleonic carriage built for the journey, one that could house a library, cooking facilities, a bed, and space for his menagerie of animals; it was pulled by four horses. I wondered whether I hadn't signed on with a traveling circus. Two servants and our luggage followed in a calèche. We departed Dover on the 25th of April and landed in Ostend that evening.

I was relieved when we checked into a hotel; I didn't relish sleeping with three large dogs, a monkey and a parrot! Eyebrows were raised when Byron asked for a single room for the both of us. He stated, with great authority, that he required the attentions of his physician at all hours of the day and night. (The concierge could not have imagined the kind of attentions he required!) As soon as we were shown the room, Byron fell like a thunderbolt upon the chambermaid. She escaped his clutches that time, but he managed to have her before our departure the following morning.

That night at the hotel in Ostend was our first together. I was rather in awe of Byron and didn't know what to expect. I could tell that he was interested in me, of course, but how that would play out remained to be seen. I had minimal experience in love-making: a number of encounters at Ampleforth with other boys my own age, and a few visits to certain available ladies in London later on. That was it. I had, up to that time, never had a lover or experienced genuine intimacy. I was sure Byron was going to take care of my deficiencies in that department. And he did. He was a wonderful lover, and surprisingly gentle. He would whisper amorously into my ear, calling me his "bonnie laddie" and even his "pretty Johnny." The intensity he brought to intimacy was something I would never experience again in that same way. I know from later experience that he treated me entirely differently than his female partners. As I said, women were objects of conquest for him. With me it was different. He still needed to be in total control, of course, but he also wanted acceptance. I found that vulnerability on his part remarkable and touching. It melted my heart.

IV.

We continued on through Belgium at an indolent pace. The carriage, which was given to breaking down, lumbered from one town to another, to Bruges (which I found very pretty), Ghent and then Brussels. Not far from that town is the field of Waterloo where, less than a year before, Napoleon's luck had finally given out on him. Byron was mostly silent as we traversed the fields. It was eerie to note that we stood on ground where 40,000 men from both sides died or were seriously wounded. There was almost no trace of the carnage left. Village urchins attempted to sell us the buttons from the uniforms of the men who had perished in the field.

His lordship was intent on avoiding French soil. After Bonaparte's abdication the monarchy was restored in France, a development which displeased Byron greatly. We headed west until we reached Cologne, then traveled south through the sublimely beautiful Rhine Valley to Switzerland. Along the way Byron did not miss an opportunity to bed any wench who crossed his path. Some were very willing partners, others needed a measure of coaxing. His powers of persuasion were nearly irresistible and he usually got what he wanted.

On more than one occasion, I was banished from our hotel room and had to spend the night in the carriage, but I didn't object. I knew that I would always share his bed again. Those were the happiest weeks of my life. In my youthful naïveté—for that is what I must call it—I thought this felicitous state would last forever. My lover was the most desired man in all of Europe and the greatest living poet in the English language to boot, and I was traveling to the most wonderful places on the continent. I was also keenly aware that half the females in England would have gladly changed places with me. I never thought it could end so soon, and with such finality.

I have a confession to make. Before leaving London, John Murray, Byron's publisher, offered me a secret deal, one I couldn't refuse. He enjoined me to keep a record of his lordship's activities. A report of Byron's personal doings would bring a fortune when made public in England. People always loved a scandal. I was to play Leporello to Byron's Don Giovanni, keeping a catalogue of the roué's conquests. (What an apt analogy that is!) Murray offered me the handsome sum of 500 pounds, more money than I had ever seen in my life. Byron never learned of this arrangement. He was made aware, however, of my own literary aspirations. I had only studied medicine because my father demanded it; he would not hear a word on me pursuing a career in literature. I begged for his lordship's guidance in my own fledgling attempts at prose and a play I was writing. I reveled in the inspiration of his work. The fact that I was now Lord Byron's *compagnon de voyage* was an incredible boon for me. I thought it was a sign from divine providence, an augury for my own eventual literary success. I was proven wrong.

V.

Finally, on the 27th of May, we reached Geneva and checked into the Hôtel d'Angleterre in Sécheron, just outside the town.

Byron had made the arrangements beforehand with the intention of staying a while. Our arrival in Geneva that day was to mark the beginning of the end for me. The nature of my relationship with Lord Byron would soon change profoundly, due to events I could not have foreseen. Neither Lord Byron nor I was aware that Percy Shelley, Mary Godwin (they were not yet married), and Mary's half sister, Claire Clairmont, had been residing at the hotel for several weeks already. Byron greatly admired Shelley's work but had never met him. He knew Claire very well. In the months before his departure from England he had had an affair with her. Claire was so determined to become his mistress that she went after him like a lynx after the fox. Byron would have offered little resistance to bedding the black-haired lass, but he soon tired of her. Claire was superficial, gossipy and demanding. What's more important, she did not possess the intellectual accomplishments that would have sustained any long-term interest in her. He dropped her, but the shameless hussy was not to be thwarted in her plans. She knew that Byron was headed for Switzerland and she managed to find out the name of the hotel in Geneva where he was going to stay. Shelley and Mary were cajoled into accompanying her to the continent. Claire (as I learned later) thought that by offering Byron an introduction to Shelley and to Mary, his estimation of her would improve. Unbeknownst to all of us, Claire had another surprise in store for Byron, one that she revealed only later.

When we checked in at the Geneva hotel, his lordship found a note from Claire waiting for him. At first he made every attempt to avoid Claire, but that proved impossible. It didn't take long before Byron gave in to Claire's dogged entreaties and he began sleeping with her again. I could tell that it wouldn't last long—and it didn't. Once again, he grew weary of her. Later on he would even forbid her from coming to the villa alone; she could only do so in the company of Shelley and Mary.

When Byron and Shelley met for the first time they bonded immediately. Here were two of the greatest intellects and poets of the age. They were in many ways opposites, but they complemented each other. Shelley was the idealistic dreamer who floated through the empyrean on the magic carpet of his ideas. There were times when I wanted to laugh out loud at his fantastical blathering, but I didn't dare. Lord Byron was the pragmatic cynic, and the ultimate narcissist. He molded the world through the potency of his words. The more time he spent with Shelley, the less interest he had in anyone else. The intellectual stimulation he received from the other poet seemed to satiate his esurient soul.

Percy Bysshe Shelley was, apart from Lord Byron himself, the most unusual man I'd ever met. He was only twenty-three at the time, five years younger than Byron, but he had already established himself as a formidable figure in literary society. Scandal pursued him like it followed Byron. In 1816 Shelley was still technically married to his first wife, Harriet. He had run off with Mary Godwin and left poor Harriet to contend with their two children alone. He was able to marry Mary only when Harriet conveniently took her own life by throwing herself into the Serpentine in Hyde Park. As I look back at it now, I realize that these high-minded individuals could be quite appalling in their behavior.

At first glance, Shelley seemed to be more of a schoolboy than a poet-philosopher. He even cultivated the impression of a youthful persona by the clothes he wore. But when one engaged him in conversation it quickly became evident that he was possessed of an extraordinary intellect. He was blond and blue-eyed and had a rather high-pitched voice. One might have thought that he was the boy/man of Byron's ideal, but I don't believe they ever indulged in any kind of carnal behavior. Their relationship was of a different sort.

Byron was gradually losing interest in me. All of us observed a shift in his personality; his unpredictable mood swings were of much concern. He could be gentle and caring one moment, then fly into a rage over nothing the next. I learned to navigate through those stormy waters and was careful not to provoke him. His displeasure often expressed itself in biting sarcasm, and I was often the object of his scorn. He became more demanding and relied more heavily on the medicines I could provide. His long conversations with Shelley must have over-stimulated his brain. Frequently, Mary sat in on these discussions of art and literature, philosophy and life. She rarely said anything, but absorbed a great deal. When I attempted to contribute anything to these conversations my opinions were immediately dismissed. Mary was a handsome woman. Byron took an interest in her, but only in a platonic way. She was one of the few women he considered an intellectual equal. He even entrusted her to make the final copies of his works before they were sent off to Murray in England. Mary was the only one of the party who showed any interest in me; she was kind and helpful. I am grateful to her for that.

VI.
June

When the arrangement at the Hôtel d'Angleterre proved to be no longer satisfactory Byron decided to rent a villa. The Shelley party had already taken a cottage in Cologny, on the south side of the lake, and Byron opted to rent the nearby Villa Diodati. It was a superb location, with a view of Lac Léman (as it is properly called) and the Jura beyond. A meadow abounding in wild flowers sloped down to the water's edge. I lived in the villa with Byron, of course, but I had become little more than a servant at that point. I was no longer his "bonnie laddie." I was now addressed as Polly and was ordered about as if I were an ordinary retainer. It was a difficult time for me. Anger, resentment and, yes, jealousy steadily grew within me. Every once in a while his lordship would show me some attention, even affection. He might run his fingers though my hair, or even kiss me. But I see now that this was calculated on his part to keep me minimally under his control. He was a master of manipulation; he knew just how to make people do what he wanted. Like so many others, men and women, I had fallen under his spell.

It was a wet and unsettled summer. Because of the daily thunderstorms, we were forced to spend a great deal of time indoors. To amuse ourselves we read and discussed various issues. Byron proposed a plan: each of us would write a ghost story. It was really a friendly rivalry between himself and Shelley—the rest of us came along for the ride. Byron did begin a story, but he soon abandoned it. The same thing happened to Shelley. I suppose they both found it difficult to create a sustained narrative: they were poets, not writers of fiction. Mary's imagination was fired by the talk of ghosts and the newly discovered powers of electricity. She had a frightening vision and shared it with Byron. He encouraged her almost daily to use that nightmare as the basis of a story and to continue working on it. At times Byron could be the best of men. I thought Mary's idea would come to nothing. Frankenstein? What a ridiculous name. I have since been proven wrong in my initial estimation of her talents. Her book has become the rage in Europe.

Claire had nothing substantial to contribute. I, on the other hand, had been hard at work writing a story. Although it was not yet finished, Byron insisted it be read aloud to everyone. He took a condescending tone in his recitation, something which did not put my work in a good light at all. When he had finished, he flung the manuscript onto a table with a gesture of utter disdain. I have not forgotten what he said: "This is rubbish, not worth the paper it is written on. Polly, stick to making your potions!" I was humiliated and boiled with anger. I craved his approval, just a kind word of encouragement. Instead, he saw fit to demean my literary efforts in this fashion. At that moment my admiration and love for him turned into pure hatred.

It was about this time that Claire informed Byron that she was pregnant with his child. He later learned that she had known of her condition in England, but did not share the news with anyone, not even Mary and Shelley. His lordship was not pleased to hear it. Inexplicably, he later forced Claire to give up the child. Allegra (so she was called) was brought to him in Venice a few years later. What did he want with a young child? I suppose he thought he could do more for her considering his wealth and position—an altruistic notion on his part—but, typically, he could not follow through with the plan in a reasonable fashion. The poor child was placed in the care of an older couple he had found and later shunted off into a convent school where she died of a fever. Poor lamb. Those who had seen the child thought it curious that she was blue-eyed and fair, just like Shelley. He adored Allegra and was grieved to part with her. She didn't resemble Byron one bit. One can draw one's own conclusions on the matter.

VII.
August

Byron and Shelley were both enthusiastic boaters. They had purchased a sailboat together and decided to take a lengthy tour of the lake on their vessel. Lac Léman is quite large, extending forty-five miles from east to west. I expected to be asked to join the party. Byron ignored my hints. I was crushed when it became clear that I was to be left behind. They were gone for two weeks. When they returned we had a bit of a celebration on the terrace. It was the first fine evening we were able to enjoy outside in a long time. Byron held forth, recounting anecdotes of their trip. Shelley was mostly silent, gazing on Byron in admiration and devotion. I was asked to prepare the libations.

My subsequent behavior was reprehensible, I will readily admit, but dear reader, you cannot imagine the rage that seethed within me. As a master of potions I concocted a special brew for his lordship and made sure he picked up the glass intended for him. I took my place on the balustrade and watched calmly as he took a sip of the doctored wine. It was not meant to kill him, of that you can be assured. I wanted to cause him some pain, just as he had aggrieved me. Byron threw the glass to the ground and exclaimed, "Polly, what have you done!" He staggered to the doorway, coughing and choking violently. I must confess that I felt some satisfaction at that moment. The sense of triumph was not to last long, however. Byron recovered by the next morning, as I knew he would. He berated me in the most violent terms and then told me to clear out. I couldn't even feign remorse. I had none. It would be the last time I ever saw him.

The following morning, before daybreak, I left the villa forever. I headed north, into the highlands. The fog-enshrouded forests enveloped me in their gloom. I realized what I had lost. Byron, for better or for worse, had been my anchor during the past few months. My own existence had been absorbed into his. Now I had nothing at all. I was an outcast. I wept bitterly.

My wanderings eventually took me to Italy, the land of my father, but nothing seemed to work out there for me. Back to England I attempted to establish a medical practice in Norwich. It failed. I drifted back to London. In 1819 I did manage to publish a story, "The Vampyre," which some attributed to Byron. That should have flattered my vanity, but it didn't. The memory of him was still too raw. I had loved him once and he treated me abominably. I should have known better, I see that now, but it is too late. Who among us can control the passions of the heart? Byron was not a man who could be loyal to anyone. He used people for his own purposes and then discarded them when it suited him.

VIII.

August 24th, 1821
London

Excessive drink has taken its toll on me. I have accrued substantial gambling debts and have no means of repaying them. My twenty-sixth birthday approaches, but I don't think I shall see that day. I have nothing to live for. The man I loved will never be mine again, and I shall never find another like him. I am weary. Once I have completed writing this account I will install myself in the well-worn armchair in the corner. There is a glass on the side table next to it, filled with a certain amber liquid. It beckons to me. I know the effects of the potion I have concocted; it will afford a quick, nearly painless end. I have ordered the maidservants not to disturb me on any account. It is dusk; the light is fading fast. I shall finish this, my last manuscript, lock it away, then drink from the stream of Lethe, my skillfully prepared brew of forgetfulness, and enter into a long and peaceful rest.

[Author's note: *John Polidori did succeed in taking his own life that day. His story, "The Vampyre," became the prototype for all subsequent vampire stories. Byron died of a fever in Greece three years later, lending his support to the noble cause of Greek liberation from the Ottomans. Shelley drowned in a boating accident off the Italian coast the following year. Mary Shelley lived a long and productive life; she never remarried. Claire worked as a governess in Russia and Germany. She outlived all of her Villa Diodati compatriots and died at the ripe old age of eighty in Florence. To the end of her life, she remained embittered about her experience with Lord Byron and the loss of her child.*]

⇒ *VOICE OF ENDANGERED SPECIES*

MOON SWALLOWS
by Stosch Sabo

Moon Swallows flit across the sunset-hued sky leaving phosphorescent wakes behind their torpedo bodies. On the night of a new moon, Moon Swallows circle upward on star-warmed thermals, reach an invisible summit, fold their wings, and dive to their death. As they fall, they leave a dusty comet trail in their suicidal wake.

People gather near farmhouse porches and park pavilions, where they stay up deep into the night to watch the Moon Swallows fall like underwater fireworks—subdued and silent yet powerful. There are many theories for the behavior, but no one knows why.

Their children, with sleepy eyes, totter to bed and dream of the Moon Swallow lights. They sleep through the yippering coyotes and the waddling raccoons. They sleep through the migration of vultures riding the sunrise rays.

When the children awake, they scamper outside and into the field searching for their Moon Swallows under the noonday sun. They find none because the birds dissipate into their own aurora as they fall. A thousand luminescent particles disperse to become Saturn rings and small stars, and a few go into the eyes of wrinkly, newborn babies who, one day, long after they are tucked away goodnight, will tightly grip the ledge of a bedroom window and peek outside with quiet eyes to watch the last of the Moon Swallows fall.

And when their newborn wrinkles grow old with age, they will still dream of the beautiful, blue-green arcs drifting in silence.

⇒ 1 BOOKSHELF

THE BOOKS-I-OWN-BUT-HAVEN'T-READ-BOOKSHELF
by Mardra Sikora

I received another book today for my imaginary bookshelf, books I own that I haven't read. Oh my, what a bookshelf this is. I need to consolidate these books, put them altogether in a pile or a shelf or a room. "Then," I tell myself. "No more new books until I read these." Or give in that I will *never* read them, and do something productive, like donate or sell them.

But alas, that is no doubt part of the reason I have not compiled and made said shelf. Sigh.

So many good books that I have both bought myself and been given as gifts. And I really do want to read them, but instead I bring home a new book that jumped off the shelf from the library, load another quick read onto my e-reader, or innocently browse and buy a book or two from the bookstore attached to the coffee shop with the best mocha in town.

These poor, neglected, good books include such titles as *Bossy Pants* by Tina Fey, a gift. I will love this book. I know I will. Tina Fey, so witty and smart, how will I stop reading once I've cracked open the book? I won't. So, I have to wait until I have an empty weekend and just binge. And when is the next empty weekend coming?

Count us In by Jason Kingsley, Mitchell Levitz and *Reviving Orphelia* by Mary Pipher and Ruth Ross, both books important to me; I know once I crack them open, I'll make notes, mark pages to research more, and dig deeply. Am I ready for that emotional commitment?

With a heavy heart and conflicted soul, I bought books at deep discounts when Borders when out of business. Finally I conceded, "It doesn't help anyone to not buy the book." Don't tell me how long ago this happened, I know... The titles are old too—*Balzac and the Little Chinese Seamstress* by Dai Sijie and Ina Rilke, *and The Time Traveler's Wife* by Audrey Niffenegger.

Then there's *Platform* by Michael Hyatt, *Tribes* by Seth Godin, and *The $100 Startup* by Chris Guillebeau—all three important for me to grow my name and business.

Books by authors I love: *Talking to Girls About Duran Duran* by Rob Sheffield, *Blue Shoe* by Anne Lamott, *Long Quiet Highway* by Natalie Goldberg, and more. I admit, more. *Many more.*

But the thing is, I need to buy the next book-club book to read before Sunday's meeting. The last time I went to the bookstore to buy the book-club book, I walked out with two more, *The End of Your Life Book Club* by Will Schwalbe and *Zen in the Art of Writing* by Ray Bradbury—no, I haven't read them yet. If I could only get my book-club to start reading from this shelf...

A READER'S MEMOIR
by Sydney Avey

I've just installed my grandmother's bookcase in my new writing studio in Arizona. I make quick decisions these days; when I packed a box of books to bring to my desert home, I chose a few that represent my interests and might intrigue the occasional guest.

My small bookcase is like a pueblo Indian ruin that has been cross-sectioned to reveal how Native Americans lived. The bottom shelf houses my husband's mystery novels. The middle collects CDs and journals. The top shelf is my treasure: used bookstore classics— Heritage reprints of *Alice in Wonderland* and *Treasure Island* that I read to my grandchildren; poetry anthologies I used in my university days; short story collections. I'm reading a short story a day and blogging about my adventures.

I have always been a reader. When I was growing up, every afternoon—my stomach grumbling because it wasn't time for dinner yet—my five-year-old self switched off the Mickey Mouse Club and chose instead to sit cross-legged on my twin bed and listen to my mother read a chapter from the *Bobbsey Twins*.

On the grammar school playground, I was the nonathletic child who spent recess leaning against a schoolyard fence trellised with honeysuckle, lost in a Nancy Drew mystery. Dodgeball held no appeal while Nancy was whipping around in her roadster having adventures.

One summer, I anchored a patio chair under the cherry tree and read all the Charles Dickens novels, one after the other, until they were all gone. That was the year I developed a sense of social justice.

To assuage my pre-adolescent angst, my mother signed a permission slip at the library allowing me full access to anything I wanted to read. I learned about the mysteries of sexual politics from *Peyton Place*, *Lady Chatterley's Lover,* and *Of Human Bondage*.

In high school, I often finished classroom assignments early. A young history teacher called me to his desk.

"You think you might like to read this?" He handed me his leather bound copy of Edgar Allan Poe. Be still my beating heart! What was more exciting, the delicious evil in those stories or a teacher's attention to the inner adult in the child?

It was natural I would major in English literature. While my roommate conjugated French verbs, I laid on the bed in the dorm reading Thomas Hardy and William Shakespeare.

"I can't believe you are getting a degree for doing what you love to do!" she would say.

Reading helped me develop confidence and an offbeat perspective. I believe people possess seven senses, and that reading is our seventh sense. Reading engages all our other faculties to help us make sense of our world. Reading helps form who we are.

Children grow up, parents pass away, lovers leave, but what we read stays with us. Stories affirm who we were, reveal who we are and challenge us on the level of who we might become.

⇒ *INTERVIEW*

THE ROLLRIGHT WITCH:
An Interview with Artist David Gosling
Interviewed by Jan Nerenberg

During the Spring 2013 semester, while in England doing research for my PhD thesis, I discovered that a natural art structure had been installed near the Rollright Stones not far from Long Compton, England. During my visit to the collection of stones, including the Whispering Knights, the King's Men, and the King Stone, I was delighted to find a rendition of Mother Shipton, standing upon the barrow mound just up from the King Stone. As there were no plaques, I began a second research project into the mysterious artist who created the sculpture, and was pleased to discover the very affable David Gosling.

Our interview conducted shortly afterward my visit to the Rollright Stones follows:

David, where did you receive your original training in art?

A: Although I left before graduation, I received my formal art training from Hornsey College of Art in England, but in the long run, I feel I learned far more from my fellow artists and from actual hands-on experience.

So you are basically self-taught. Have you always wanted to work in art?

A: Yes, I've always been drawn to the creation of things.

What was the first piece of art you installed?
A: That's a difficult question as my installations go back quite a long way. I started environmental art though after making a piece in a local park in Banbury, out of natural-found material. It was made with dried grass/stems woven into the trees. I decided then and there that this was going to be my future path. I learned tapestry weaving in Edinburgh, where I lived for ten years.

Things They Carry 142

David tell us a bit about your early successes?

A. I exhibited and sold pastel drawings of Scottish landscapes in Edinburgh, and also created willow sculptures for various councils.

I've been to your website (davidgosling.com) and have seen the living willow bower you installed in your garden. It reminded me of something I saw at Anne Hathaway's home in Stratford upon Avon.

Of all your installations, David, which would you say was your favorite, and perhaps you'd tell us why you choose installation art as your mode of artistic expression?

A. I much prefer the land art pieces, which are made for and quite often *from* the natural environment. They have a spiritual quality for me. You could say that they are unclaimed by commercial value. As to my choice of installation art, I like the freedom of space the outdoors gifts to me. I can create without borders and edges limiting my creativity.

David, your art is not just an expression of self and how you see the world, it is also a statement of your love for nature.

But, may I ask, how do you feel knowing that your installation art is temporary, rather than a more traditional art form, which lives on past the artist for hundreds of years?

A. Well, as I see it, we are all transient anyway. Somebody once said to me that my work has been reclaimed by nature... I like that. It is satisfying to me.

Before we move on to the Rollright Witch, can you share with our readers which was your favorite project and why?

A. My favorite projects were the ones that I quietly made in the natural world, photographed and then dismantled. Some were never seen by anyone but me. However, as satisfying as these are, they do not pay the bills. They are, nonetheless, good for teaching when I share them with interested students.

David, now we come to the part of the interview that caused me to locate you in the first place—the Rollright Witch. How did the idea for the Rollright Witch come about?

A. I was taken for a drive to the Rollright Stones by my son a couple of years back and he thought it a good idea to make a sculpture there, which I agreed, so I contacted George of the Rollrights, who also agreed. The wood was donated from the Compton Verney estate and is in fact trees from an avenue of Wellingtonia's, which had been "dead wooded." A little earlier we had made a living willow structure for them. Wellingtonia is a hard wood and has a lot of twisty bits, perfect for constructing sculptures, and also has a good color. It was made on a long weekend with the help of my two sons, Adam and Luke and a friend, Rob. It was constructed with nails and a little 2.5 fencing wire and most of the wood was trimmed after construction with a chainsaw. It was just built up by us, branch by branch, on site, finding the appropriate shape and angle of wood to fit. We had a great weekend.

Did you know of Mother Shipton and her mythic connection to the stones?

A. I actually learned of her when I was researching the idea of creating a sculpture at the Rollrights. After I worked on the initial concept, the idea of using natural wood just came to me while making the original sketch.

Have you or the Rollright Trust considered making your witch a permanent feature at the stones?

A. I hope not, I like the idea of change. Although they are talking of moving the sculpture and I told them that we would restore the work if they did so.

I, for one, David, hope that they leave her right where she is. I sat for hours just contemplating her and thought she was brilliantly placed, wand outstretched just by the King Stone. At a certain angle, one can almost see a face. She was very inspiring for my upcoming book.

Things They Carry 145

David, as we talked about your process and installations, you say that you don't keep a common-book or history of each project. You've also mentioned that sometimes you apply to do an installation and sometimes you are approached. Once you have started, what is your process?

A. Mostly discussions and lots of drawings. Then, of course, one has to come to an agreement and pass approvals with the contracting party of what I see in my vision for the finished work.

David, I'd like to say thank you so very much for the time you've taken to share your art with the world and for your generosity in giving your time for this interview. I understand that you are now looking into a well-earned retirement, but one last question. How would you like to be remembered?

A. That's easy. I'd like to be remembered as the artist who worked from the soul.

(Photos used with permission. © David Gosling, Jan Nerenberg)

⇒ *AUTHOR BOOK REVIEWS*

LEAVE OF ABSENCE
by Tanya Peterson

Seek first to understand. Although I didn't know it consciously at the time, I internalized this mantra a long time ago, back in elementary school. It was more than a mere mantra, actually. It became my personal lodestar on my life's journey.

As a child, I watched from the side as the other children squabbled and harassed each other in class or on the playground. I witnessed the tears that resulted, and I wondered why people acted the way they did. Why did pain have to exist in the world? Why did people have to suffer? I was too young to understand the complexities of human behavior, but I was not too young to imagine.

I went to college to become a teacher, perhaps in some way to seek answers to those questions. While I loved to explore history and literature and world language with my students, I found myself looking beyond the teaching to see *whom* I was teaching. Why did one kid fail and one succeed? Why did some adolescents treat others well, but some treat others poorly, and vise versa? As I sought to understand them, my interest grew in becoming a counselor.

Flash forward a few more years. Many things converged at once to lead me down the path of understanding. In no particular order, I experienced the following: the decline and end of my marriage; a traumatic brain injury in a car accident; acceptance into graduate school; the eventual reconciliation of my relationship with my ex-husband; a series of hospitalizations in a behavioral health center; single parenthood; an absolute love for my graduate program in counseling, and the ability to thrive, learn, excel despite external life stressors; opportunities to apply my counseling degree in service to others; a very accurate diagnosis of bipolar disorder. It was a messy time.

Perhaps the two most profound impacts on me from this period of time were my studies in psychology and counseling, and time spent at a behavioral health hospital. I learned much about the *whys* of human behavior, and how to be helpful to people. In meeting other patients at the behavioral health hospital, I found that the most important thing people wanted was to be understood.

We all have stories of pain and suffering, joy and triumph. Many of the people I encountered suffered not only from personal mental illness, but from the harsh judgments of others. My journey taught me that much of the mistreatment humans sometimes inflict upon each other, comes not from a desire to be cruel, but from a lack of understanding. Certainly, if we could spend a moment in another person's shoes, we'd have a glimpse of what life might be like for someone suffering from mental illness.

My path in life has been littered with stereotypes, stigmas, prejudices and misunderstandings. Throughout it all, I maintained a habit (maybe a coping mechanism) of crafting stories, real and imagined, about my experiences. Combining my passions, education, life-experience, and my love of writing, *Leave of Absence* was born.

In this novel, Penelope Baker wrestles with schizophrenia and the devastating impact its had on her once happy and successful life. Penelope's fiancé, William Vaile, desperately seeks to convince her that she's worth loving. A second story is told simultaneously about Oliver Graham, a man who is utterly bereft and laden with guilt in the aftermath of the traumatic deaths of his wife and son. Readers join them on their tumultuous journey through pain, struggle, and triumphs.

Leave of Absence is set at the fictitious Airhaven Behavioral Health Center, but mirrors some of my own experiences. Readers might relate with the real-life experience, like this one, where Oliver is hospitalized:

Oliver was already awake at six forty-five on Saturday morning, so he heard the tech in the day area as she progressed from door to door, waking the patients. Every morning it was the same: The sound of knuckles rapping on a wooden door. Knock, knock, knock. Three times in quick succession. Oliver wondered about that. Why three quick taps? Was it part of some handbook for dealing with people with mental health issues? Maybe it was for patients with obsessive-compulsive disorder. Or maybe the night techs, who did this as the last part of their shift, had OCD themselves. Or was three a magic number that would summon a magic genie, who would come poofing out of something and cure everyone? If that were the case, it wasn't working.

Kirkus Reviews said of *Leave of Absence*: "Peterson succeeds in demystifying the world of psychiatric care and challenging the stigma that continues to surround mental health." *US Review of Books* wrote, "The author helps strip away the surface stereotypes associated with those who suffer from PTSD and schizophrenia to show the real people underneath." *Portland Book Review* had this to say: "In a sordid way, [Peterson] puts us all in the place of the suffering so that we may better understand how to approach what we cannot relate."

And that returns me to my quest for human understanding. At one point in the story, Penelope laments, as tears spill down her cheeks, "I'm not the same anymore. I had to quit the job I loved. At first, I thought I could just take a leave of absence, just a little break to get better enough to go back. I had to quit completely, and now I'm just a loser."

My goal in writing *Leave of Absence* was to portray the humanity behind the mental illness, to help people understand the Penelopes and Olivers of the world.

No one is a loser.

BIRTHING MY NOVEL
by Holly Lorincz

The pregnancy was rough—unexpected, really. While I occasionally daydreamed of writing a novel, I didn't have the time to write for myself, the freedom to expend my creative juices on any of my own projects. At the time I was a high school English and speech teacher and a debate coach. My inspiration and energy belonged to my students. But then one of the adorable fourteen-year-olds smeared her ebola-swineflu-black-plague-laden snot bubbles into her much-handled college-ruled notebook paper, and handed in an essay with a side of mononucleosis. Mono quietly morphed into chronic Epstein Barr. So, yeah. Suddenly I had free time.

Thus, my novel, *Smart Mouth,* was born. At first I wrote to keep depression and an identity crisis at bay, but seven chapters in, I started writing in order to publish. And I mean publish for-realsies, with a traditional publishing house. I had no intention of hocking my book like a car, trying to sell through self-publishing, on the Inter-webs. Oh, silly me. I should have known I was being stupid when I did it myself. My agent still swears a traditional publishing house will pick up *Smart Mouth,* but I think he's been blinded to reality by my smart-alecky prose, or he's confusing me with the multiple Lorincz's in his client roster. I'm not saying this because I no longer believe my book is worthy—I'm saying this because I work in publishing. The magical three months after he sent proposals out have reached an editor's desk and come and gone without receiving a nicely worded rejection letter from any of them.

I'm not quite sure how it happened exactly, but I suddenly find myself on the Ebook Road. Clearly, once I make up my mind, it means nothing. Because of this choice, to market online, I've once again lost my hard-earned free time. All 126 of my friends that own Kindles or Nooks have bought it... so now what? Ugh. I wish I had the energy to do whatever it is that I need to do to really make a go of this thing. Blog tours, radio shows, podcasts, newspaper interviews, finding reviewers, learning the ins and outs of the shifty underpinnings in the land of Amazon... jeez, I need an intern, preferably one who is technologically saavy, understands market-needs, and can type 150 words a minute. You know, a thirteen-year-old. As I stutter-step my way through *Marketing,* the Holly

Lorincz Way, I find am asked to address the same questions over and over. (There are two in particular I have come to abhor.) "Is *Smart Mouth* autobiographical?" And "What genre does your book fall into?"

Let me tackle the autobiographical issue first, including a sketch of the book, and why this question has come to irritate me so much. First off, *Smart Mouth*, a dramatic comedy, is told from the point of view of three characters. The main voice, though, is that of Addy, a twenty-three-year-old seeking a place in the adult world while trying to overcome her stultifying shyness and fear of conflict. She decides that moving from the city to a small town in order to teach high school English is the best bet to slingshot her into maturity and confidence. The book opens on her first miserable day in the classroom, ending with the administration forcing her to take on the coaching position of a new debate team. She's about to crack and run, but the desperation of her students keeps her tethered, barely. This is Addy's coming-of-age story; it is also a David versus Goliath tale, describing the importance of the battles that her rural, rag-tag team engage in against the bigger, richer and entitled schools, while they each try to find their voices. It isn't until Addy can stand up and let her *smart mouth* fly that she can help her charges. If she gives up, or fails, so do they.

So. Addy. Is she me? And who cares, right? Wrong. For some reason, people *really* seem to care. I was an English teacher and speech coach at a rural school for fifteen years, so they (editors/agents) believe this is some kind of veiled memoir or tell-all expose. Yes, I used my experiences and my reactions and those of my peers to help develop a storyline. Yes, I definitely culled characteristics and quirks from teachers and students I have known over the years. BUT, of course, I'm a writer, which means I'm a storyteller, and not one incident or character in the book would appear remotely similar to the real-life-experience of those involved. I've never once had someone say, "Oh, yeah, I remember when that happened." I think all writers take a bit of reality, break it down, rebuild it, reshape it, rename it and *voila*—something new has been born. Hell, life is interesting.

Anyway, I've come to terms with saying for the thousandth time, *no, this isn't about me. I've never been shy; these characters don't exist.* What bothers me the most, though, are the professional editors or people in the publishing biz who read my bio, and then the story blurb, and immediately assume my main character is going to be shallow and unimaginative because I'm "really" writing about me. My answer to that is, most readers will not know me so why would they think I'm writing about myself? I've considered changing my bio to declare myself a prostitute or a construction worker. Problem solved.

A much bigger, more impactful issue is the genre delineation. I didn't set out to create a woman-centric book, nor do I believe the end product falls into the genre of women's fiction. However, every publishing expert insists that because the main character is a twenty-three-year-old woman no man will ever want to read my book. Now, granted, *Smart Mouth* is no amazing piece of literary fiction like *She's Come Undone* or *Book of Ruth* (both with young female leads), but neither is it Chic Lit. The story has depth and breadth, and deals with universal issues, often with humor but always with sincerity. Again, I'm in no way saying I've created the great American novel here—I just hate to have this story be pigeonholed in such a way that half the reading population is instantly sloughed away because of an ill-conceived genre label. I'm well aware of the statistics, that *supposedly* men in general don't read from the point of view of a woman character, unless maybe it's non-fiction. But, jeez, doesn't this kind of gender labeling keep some from even trying? And, from a selfish point of view, doesn't that keep male teachers, or shy males, or males struggling with adulthood, or males who like to laugh, from buying my "girly" book.

In the end, writing a novel is gratifying. Selling it is a whole other story.

⇒ *WISDOMGRAMS*

To: The Fearful
From: B. Wesley Martin, Lancaster, Pennsylvania
While hiking the Appalachian Trail, October 2010: In a moment of absolute clarity I noticed that our lives are like those of leaves on a tree whose true goal is the growth of the greater Earth. Then, in the winter of our lives we will fall gently to the ground and, in doing so, will somehow replenish life. Why fear death when it is merely a continuation of life?

To: Myself and Family
From: The Lovely Woman at the Airport
We are all rich, wealthier than we can ever imagine, because we are alive. You take in the world every moment you breathe. A gift from the universe. Just think of that. We breathe in over a hundred thousand times a day. Now... consider your wealth.

To: Rich & Famous
From: Crony Clin, vyas1981.blogspot.in
Either wealth makes you famous or fame makes you wealthy.

To: Aspiring Writers
From: God via Sydney Avey, SydneyAvey.com
Ask *Me* for open doors. As you go through, hold the door open for someone behind you.

To: Seekers
From: A Fellow Seeker (Alison Thalhammer, alisonthalhammer.com)
Enough is enough when enough is all you know; now is always now, and can never be more or less than that. When later is now, later will still be later and now will be then. Now. Forever. Enough. 'Til no more. 'Til enough is not enough, but, too much.

To: Each individual
From: Carlylrkn5, www.silverpen.org
Be brave, not fearless. Be wise, but not too serious. Speak with compassion, but don't be speechless. Lend an ear to listen, in no attempt to fit together their broken pieces. Most of all, speak for the unspoken, and be honest, but not entirely open.

Things They Carry

⇒ *HOMOGRAPHS*

HOMOGRAPIES
by Richard Kostelanetz

When on trial, don't court officers of the court.

Measure your front yards not in feet but in yards.

Only those trained in dance can dance a dance.

He could lead if he would get the lead out of his shoes.

His stomach full, the soldier decided to desert his dessert in the desert.

Every period of history he could summarize within a single sentence ending with a period.

Irregularities in the evening weather are evening out.
Incense can incense delicate sensibilities.

I wonder in awe about the wonder of the universe.

On the spur of the moment he jabbed his horse with his spur.

May I write a play about child's play.

Only within a steel safe would my gold be safe.

How can I intimate this to my most intimate friend?

The artist is drawing a man drawing water.

homograph | ˈhäməˌgraf; ˈhōmə- | noun
Each of two or more words spelled the same but not necessarily pronounced the same and having different meanings and origins.

⇒ ARTIST VIEW OF OUR WORLD

CONSTITUTION AVENUE
by Brett Busang

Acrylic on masonite, 20″ x 24″, © 2005, Brett Busang

Capitol Hill is treasured for its historic architecture. Sometimes I find its devotion idolatrous; at other times, it seems absolutely right—a good cause for an already-busy population. Back in the Fifties, a huge swath of the Hill was threatened, but, after a groundswell of publicity and the sort of behind-the-scenes politicking for which Washingtonians are justly renowned, local activists put a stop to the highway that would have taken the hide off their neighborhood. Some of the heroes of that era are with us today, still banging the drum, ready to mount the podium for a shotgun house or public fountain. The crusaders among us make it possible to keep the things we want—even if *we* do little else but talk.

East Capitol Street is the Commonwealth Avenue of Capitol Hill. It's been, among other things, the backdrop to history. People walked up "East Cap" to hear Lincoln deliver the second inaugural of his presidency. (They started out in the rain, but came back in the sunshine.) Some of the cottages from that era are still among us, jockeying for space amidst their sprawling neighbors. As East Capitol walks its ruler-straight path, these cottages give way to prideful Victorians which yield the baton, further up, to limestone-sided castles. Sprinkled among these are corner stores and unlikely beauty parlors.

Yet it's the adjacent streets that embody the spirit of *The Hill*, which was made one brick at a time by people who were on a budget. The famous people don't really count. It's the folk who used to carry satchels and briefcases—and noodle around with their iPads—who are its soldiers and statesmen. They tend the gardens, sweep the sidewalks, and water the lawns. After fixing a porch that has sagged for years, they come out and paint it. They attend the dreadfully dull meetings that determine whether better streetlights will be put in—or get a larger police presence in areas that are considered dicey.

Such people are responsible for the way Constitution Avenue, and all the unremarkable-looking streets and neighborhood spurs, look today. And I think someone should thank them.

SKULLS WITH RED STRIPES
by Ira Joel Haber

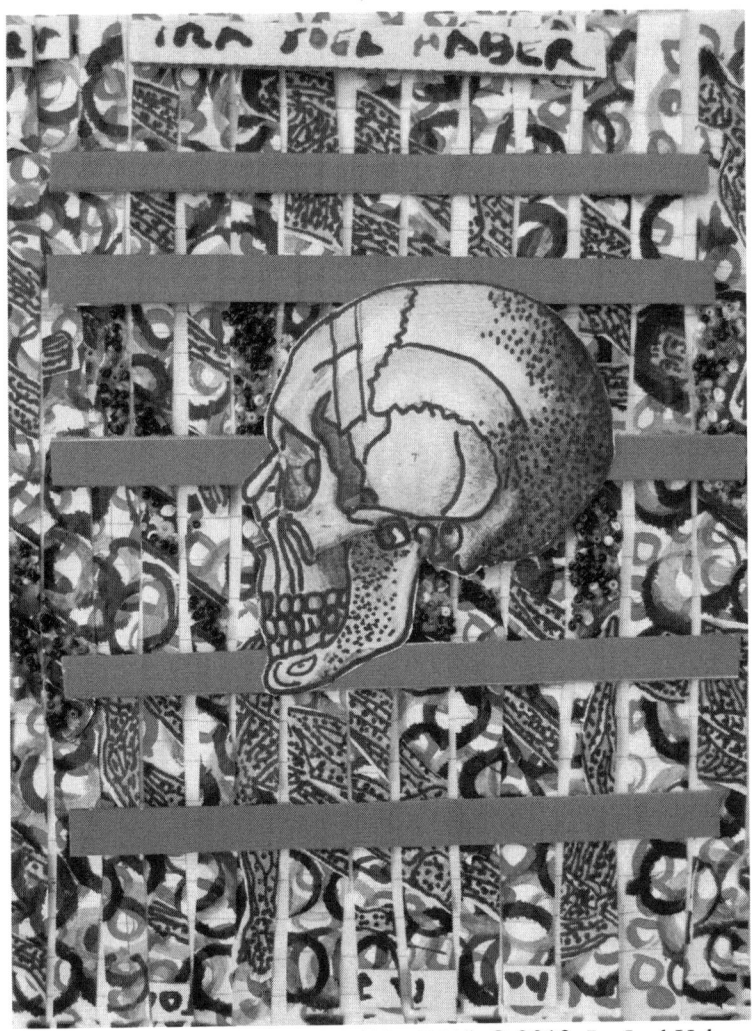

Mixed on notebook paper, 9 3/4″ x 7 ½″, © 2013, Ira Joel Haber

BANANALAND
by Christopher Woods

Black & white photo, © 2012, Christopher Woods

HEAD FLOATING ON GROUND
by Ivan de Monbrison

Original photography, 16"x 12", © 2013, Ivan de Monbrison, Paris

SUN HAT
by Amelia Jane Nierenberg

Oil Painting, 2013, ©Amelia Nierenberg

THE MUSE
by Cassie M. Seinuk

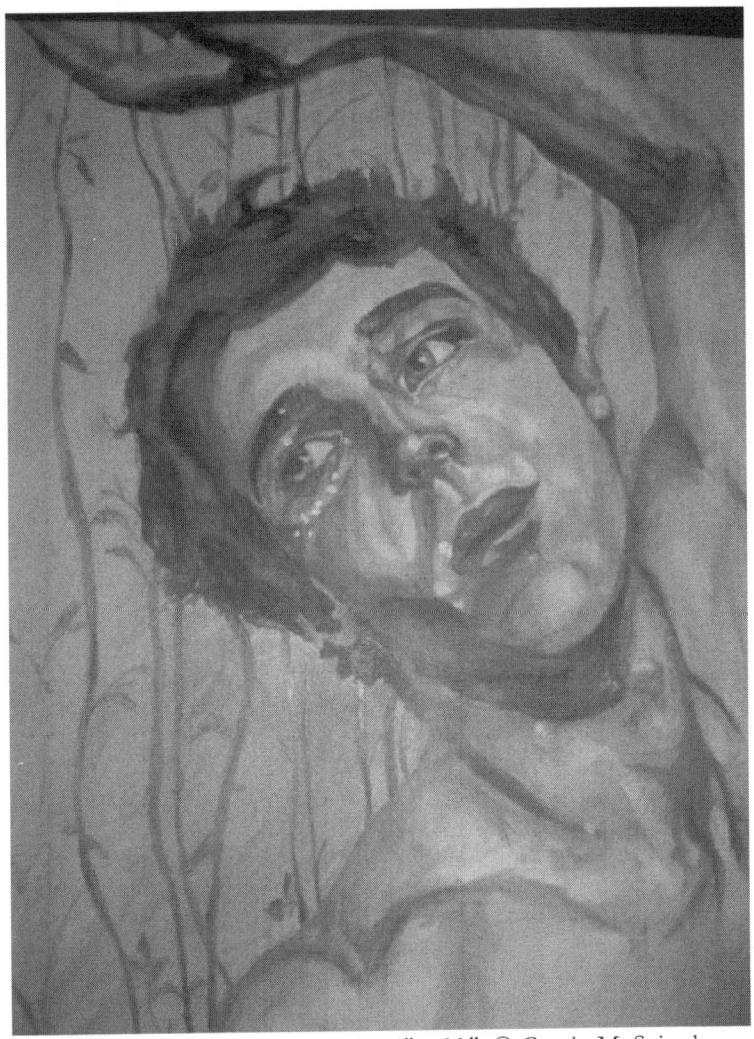

Aquarelle on drawing board, 16" x 20", © Cassie M. Seinuk

JACK KEROUAC
by Loren Kantor

Black Ink Woodcut Print, 5″ x 6″, 2012, © Loren Kantor

HONEY DO
by Patricia Merlino

Color photo, 2013, © Patricia Merlino

⇒ *SERIALIZATION*

THE STORY OF DOCTOR DOLITTLE
Chapter 4: A Message From Africa
by Hugh Lofting

That winter was a very cold one. And one night in December, when they were all sitting round the warm fire in the kitchen, and the Doctor was reading aloud to them out of books he had written himself in animal-language, the owl, Too-Too, suddenly said, "Sh! What's that noise outside?"

They all listened; and presently they heard the sound of some one running. Then the door flew open and the monkey, Chee-Chee, ran in, badly out of breath.

"Doctor!" he cried, "I've just had a message from a cousin of mine in Africa. There is a terrible sickness among the monkeys out there. They are all catching it—and they are dying in hundreds. They have heard of you, and beg you to come to Africa to stop the sickness."

"Who brought the message?" asked the Doctor, taking off his spectacles and laying down his book.

"A swallow," said Chee-Chee. "She is outside on the rain-butt."

"Bring her in by the fire," said the Doctor. "She must be perished with the cold. The swallows flew South six weeks ago!"

So the swallow was brought in, all huddled and shivering; and although she was a little afraid at first, she soon got warmed up and sat on the edge of the mantelpiece and began to talk.

When she had finished the Doctor said,

"I would gladly go to Africa—especially in this bitter weather. But I'm afraid we haven't money enough to buy the tickets. Get me the money-box, Chee-Chee."

So the monkey climbed up and got it off the top shelf of the dresser.

There was nothing in it—not one single penny!

"I felt sure there was twopence left," said the Doctor.

"There WAS," said the owl. "But you spent it on a rattle for that badger's baby when he was teething."

"Did I?" said the Doctor. "Dear me, dear me! What a nuisance money is, to be sure! Well, never mind. Perhaps if I go down to the

Things They Carry 164

seaside I shall be able to borrow a boat that will take us to Africa. I knew a seaman once who brought his baby to me with measles. Maybe he'll lend us his boat—the baby got well."

So early the next morning the Doctor went down to the seashore. And when he came back he told the animals it was all right—the sailor was going to lend them the boat.

Then the crocodile and the monkey and the parrot were very glad and began to sing, because they were going back to Africa, their real home. And the Doctor said,

"I shall only be able to take you three—with Jip the dog, Dab-Dab the duck, Gub-Gub the pig and the owl, Too-Too. The rest of the animals, like the dormice and the water-voles and the bats, they will have to go back and live in the fields where they were born till we come home again. But as most of them sleep through the Winter, they won't mind that—and besides, it wouldn't be good for them to go to Africa."

So then the parrot, who had been on long sea-voyages before, began telling the Doctor all the things he would have to take with him on the ship.

"You must have plenty of pilot-bread," she said. "*Hard tack* they call it. And you must have beef in cans—and an anchor."

"I expect the ship will have its own anchor," said the Doctor.

"Well, make sure," said Polynesia. "Because it's very important. You can't stop if you haven't got an anchor. And you'll need a bell."

"What's that for?" asked the Doctor.

"To tell the time by," said the parrot. "You go and ring it every half-hour and then you know what time it is. And bring a whole lot of rope—it always comes in handy on voyages."

Then they began to wonder where they were going to get the money from to buy all the things they needed.

"Oh, bother it! Money again," cried the Doctor. "Goodness! I shall be glad to get to Africa where we don't have to have any! I'll go and ask the grocer if he will wait for his money till I get back— No, I'll send the sailor to ask him."

So the sailor went to see the grocer. And presently he came back with all the things they wanted.

Then the animals packed up; and after they had turned off the water so the pipes wouldn't freeze, and put up the shutters, they closed the house and gave the key to the old horse who lived in the stable. And when they had seen that there was plenty of hay in the loft to last the horse through the Winter, they carried all their luggage down to the seashore and got on to the boat.

The Cat's-meat-Man was there to see them off; and he brought a large suet-pudding as a present for the Doctor because, he said he had been told, you couldn't get suet-puddings in foreign parts.

As soon as they were on the ship, Gub-Gub, the pig, asked where the beds were, for it was four o'clock in the afternoon and he wanted his nap. So Polynesia took him downstairs into the inside of the ship and showed him the beds, set all on top of one another like book-shelves against a wall.

"Why, that isn't a bed!" cried Gub-Gub. "That's a shelf!"

"Beds are always like that on ships," said the parrot. "It isn't a shelf. Climb up into it and go to sleep. That's what you call 'a bunk.'"

"I don't think I'll go to bed yet," said Gub-Gub. "I'm too excited. I want to go upstairs again and see them start."

"Well, this is your first trip," said Polynesia. "You will get used to the life after a while." And she went back up the stairs of the ship, humming this song to herself:

I've seen the Black Sea and the Red Sea;
I rounded the Isle of Wight;
I discovered the Yellow River,
And the Orange too by night.
Now Greenland drops behind again,
And I sail the ocean Blue.
I'm tired of all these colors, Jane,
So I'm coming back to you.

They were just going to start on their journey, when the Doctor said he would have to go back and ask the sailor the way to Africa.

But the swallow said she had been to that country many times and would show them how to get there.

So the Doctor told Chee-Chee to pull up the anchor and the voyage began.

⇒ BIOGRAPHIES

You've read them. Now support them. Go to their website, become a fan, buy their wares. Support artists—they love sharing their work.

Victoria Boynton teaches creative writing at SUNY Cortland. She publishes essays on women and writing as well as poems and stories, including a chapbook with Stockport Flats Press, *Contraptions* (2009) and poems in *Verse, Harper Palate, The Comstock Review, Calyx, Margie, Spillway, Heliotrope* and other magazines.

Ivan de Monbrison was born in Paris in 1969 from a French-Protestant father and an Egyptian-Muslim mother, both mixed with Jewish origins. His interest in art can be linked to a very liberal artistic education, where African and Oceania arts were in the center of his interests. This left him with a desire to pursue the question of what art meant in the old days, and how can this be dealt with in our modern and absurd world of thriving technology. Is art religious? Thus in what way can it still be in a non-sacralised world? Chasing the human figure in a distorted way, like Bacon and Giacometti did in the past, has appeared for him the best way for this non-religious "spiritual" quest. In the recent years, Ivan's work has been shown in many countries. artmajeur.com/blackowl

Jennifer Falkner is the editor of *Circa: A Journal of Historical Fiction*. Some of her writing has recently appeared in *THEMA, Vintage Script* and *The Copperfield Review*, among other places. She lives in Ottawa, Canada.

Ira Joel Haber was born and lives in Brooklyn. He's a sculptor, painter, book dealer, photographer and teacher. His work has been seen in numerous group-shows in the USA and Europe. His work is in the collections of *the Whitney Museum of American Art*, New York University, *the Guggenheim Museum, the Hirshhorn Museum* and *The Albright-Knox Art Gallery*. His paintings, drawings, photographs and collages have been published in over 100 online and print magazines. He has received three National Endowment for the Arts Fellowships, two Pollock-Krasner grants, the Adolph Gottlieb Foundation grant. He teaches art at the United Federation of Teachers Retiree Program. irajoelcinemagebooks.blogspot.com

Major Christopher J. Heatherly is a career US Army officer and veteran of combat operations in Afghanistan and Iraq. He holds master's degrees from the University of Oklahoma and the School of Advanced Military Studies. His previous publishing credits include *Armchair General, The Austin Statesman, The Peoria Journal Star, Bluestreak, The Journal of Military Experience–Volume II*, and *Military Officer* magazine.

Catherine Jagoe is a translator and writer, originally from the UK and now living in Wisconsin. She has a PhD in Spanish Literature from the University of Cambridge and is the author or translator of six books, including two novels, *That Bringas Woman* by Benito Pérez Galdós (Everyman, 1996) and *My Name is Light* by Elsa Osorio (Bloomsbury, 2003), and a work of literary criticism, *Ambiguous Angels: Gender in the Novels of Galdós* (University of California Press, 1994). Poems from her collection *Casting Off* (Parallel Press, 2007) were featured on *The Writer's Almanac* and *Poetry Daily*. She is a contributor to Wisconsin Public Radio's *Wisconsin Life* series.

Gail Jeidy has been a writer throughout her career (freelance journalism, TV and business) and has focused on dramatic writing in multiple forms over the past ten years. Her writing credits include regional and national magazines, newspapers, literary journals (*Stymie, Quiddity, Common Thought, Mason's Road*, among others), the Prairie Home Companion website, and short-listed in several recent screenplay competitions. Gail earned a BS from the University of Wisconsin, and completed an MFA from Lesley University. Gail lives in Portland, Oregon, with her family and teaches script writing at Portland Community College. gailjeidy.blogspot.com

Loren Kantor is a Los Angeles-based woodcut and linocut artist. He worked in the movie industry for twenty years as a screenwriter and assistant director. He's been carving woodcut images for the past five years. He's enthralled with vintage movies and classic American authors. He loves the old, the antiquated, the forgotten and neglected elements of life. He looks to the past for wisdom and inspiration and through woodcutting, he integrates an archaic process with today's digital universe. Where digital imagery

and sounds are ethereal and cannot be touched, Loren relishes the tactile nature of carved wood and hand-pressed ink prints. He hopes that through his carving he can pay homage to his cultural ancestors and artistic forerunners from the past.
woodcuttingfool.blogspot.com

erica l. kaufman lives in Providence, Rhode Island in an old, tilted red house with her needy cat and her less-needy husband. Originally from New Hampshire, she earned her BFA from Emerson College in Writing, Literature, and Publishing and in June 2013 earned her MFA in Writing for Young People at Lesley University.

Shirley Kuo is an aspiring poet currently residing in California. Her work has been published by the *Young Adult Review Network, The Cuckoo Quarterly, The Toucan Magazine*, and others. She breathes for books, early sunrises, and thunderstorms.

Holly Lorincz lives on the Oregon coast with her family, and works for MacGregor Literary as an editing and publishing consultant. Before Mac Lit, she was the editor of a literary magazine, and then a nationally recognized instructor, teaching literature, journalism, and speech and writing, at the high school and college level. Please visit her author's page for excerpts from her current novel, *The Same River, Twice*. She also offers free children's books at hollylorincz.wordpress.com. Or visit literaryconsulting.com.

Cristina Mendez is a high-school student with a deep passion for social activism and justice. She spends her time writing thought-provoking essays, short stories and poems about the world today. Cristina finds inspiration in the issues of everyday life and in those faced in history.

Patricia Merlino is an Adjunct Professor for Arcadia University. She holds a MS in Computer Science from Nova Southeastern University. When not engaged in the technical, she is a street photographer with a unique perspective photographing summer life in Southern New Jersey. Since 2006, her work has centered on a themed collection of a local Italian Feast and Carnival. More of her work can be viewed on her website sjstreetphotography.com.

John Mueter is an educator, pianist, vocal coach, composer and writer. His fiction has been accepted by various literary journals, including: *Freedom Forge Press, Twisted Endings, Wilde Oats Journal, Writers Haven, Biblioteca Alexandrina, Haiku Journal*. His opera *Everlasting Universe*, about Lord Byron at the Villa Diodati, was premiered in 2007. He currently teaches at the University of Kansas.

Amelia Jane Nierenberg is a Junior at the Ethical Culture Fieldston School in New York where she is Editor of Fieldston's art magazine, *Dope Ink*. She has participated in Les Tapies (affiliated with TASIS), the Art Studio Workshop Intensive Summer European Trip, and the Early College Program at the School of the Art Institute of Chicago. She received five Regional Honorable Mentions, three Regional Silver Keys and three Regional Gold Keys from the Scholastic Art and Writing Awards. Her artwork has been shown in the Fieldston Summer Show, the NYC Scholastic Regional Awards and #artbecause. Her written work has been published in: *Slash of Red, Torrid Literature, Ruminate Magazine,* and *Black Fox Literary Magazine*.

Lee Passarella is a founding member and senior literary editor of *Atlanta Review* and acted as editor-in-chief of *FutureCycle Poetry* and Coreopsis Books. His poetry has appeared in *Chelsea, Cream City Review, Louisville Review, The Sun, Antietam Review, Journal of the American Medical Association, The Formalist, Cortland Review,* and many other periodicals. Recent publications include *Stickman Review, FutureCycle Poetry,* and *Rock & Sling*. "Swallowed up in Victory," Passarella's long narrative poem based on the American Civil War, was published by White Mane Books in 2002. In addition, he has published two other books of poetry: *The Geometry of Loneliness* (David Roberts Books) and *Sight-Reading Schumann* (Pudding House Publications).

John Poblocki did not serve in the Vietnam War. Instead, he received a draft deferment, finished his undergraduate degree in civil engineering at Worcester Polytechnic Institute and then received a Masters degree in community planning at the University of Rhode Island. He is the proud father of three wonderfully creative adult offspring and one out-of-control bamboo plant. He and his wife, Maria, live in Forest Hills, New York. While his lifelong passion has been writing, he has spent much of his career in the commercial real estate industry. He still thinks often about the war, how it affected a generation and how little the present generation knows about this war.

Jeff Rasley is a graduate of the University of Chicago, A.B. magna cum laude, Phi Beta Kappa; Indiana University School of Law, J.D. cum laude, Moot Court and Indiana Law Review; Christian Theological Seminary, M.Div. magna cum laude, co-valedictorian and Faculty Award Scholar. Rasley has been admitted to the Indiana US District Court and US Supreme Court Bars. He is currently partner in Knowledge Capture Publishing and Editing, president of the Basa Village Foundation USA Inc., and US liaison for the Nepal-based Himalayan expedition company, Adventure GeoTreks Ltd. Rasley is the author of seven books and has published numerous articles and photos in academic and mainstream periodicals, including *Newsweek, Chicago Magazine, ABA Journal, Family Law Review, Pacific Magazine, Indy's Child, The Journal of Communal Societies, The Chrysalis Reader, Faith & Fitness Magazine, Friends Journal,* and *Real Travel Adventures International Magazine.*

Stosch Sabo is an engineer in Texas. He studied engineering and writing at Winona State University, and his work has also appeared in *RED OCHRE LiT.*

Cassie M. Seinuk is a Boston-based playwright, AEA stage manager, and visual artist. Her plays have been seen nationally including: New York, Boston, Chicago, and Florida. She is the co-founder of Interim Writers, a playwright's collective that produces monthly readings in Cambridge, and is part of their Accomplice Writers' Group. She has her MFA in Creative Writing for Stage and Screen from Lesley University. For more info and artwork visit cassiemseinuk.com.

Duke Trott was born in Birmingham Michigan and graduated in 2013 from Eckerd College with a degree in creative writing and literature. His work has been published by *American Athenaeum* and *The Bare Knuckle Review*. Some of his favorite writers include Natasha Trethewey, A.R Ammons, and Galway Kinnell.

Mardra Sikora recently retired from her position of President of Wright Printing Company in Omaha, NE to pursue publication of her first novel, *The Innocent Prince*. Her day-to-day and bigger dreams are found online at mardrasikora.com.

Robert Blake Truscott's work has appeared over the last three decades in over forty-five literary journals including: *The Virginia Quarterly Review, Nimrod, The Mississippi Review, Sou'wester, The Greenfield Review, The California Quarterly,* and *The Literary Review,* among many others. Anthologies include: *In The West of Ireland,* and *The Hampden-Sydney Review Anthology,* among others. Mr. Truscott was the poetry editor for more than a decade with *Stone Country,* before the journal ceased publication. He is a graduate of the Johns Hopkins Writing Seminars, and teaches writing as a distance-learning instructor. Mr. Truscott was the Assistant Director and Writing Specialist for The Douglass/Cook College writing Center at Rutgers University for seven years and was a Senior Communications Consultant for *SWG Consulting* in New York City for fifteen years. He is currently married and lives in Colorado in the resplendent shadow of Pikes Peak.

Susan Levi Wallach is a freelance copyeditor in South Carolina. Her poem, "Catalogue," appeared in the summer issue of *The Moth*. Her novel, *Flasher*, was a finalist in the 2012 Faulkner-Wisdom Creative Writing Competition. She has an MFA from Vermont College of Fine Arts.

Christopher Woods is a writer, teacher and photographer who lives in Texas. For gallery, visit: christopherwoods.zenfolio.com. About the photograph: "I am drawn to the carny world and the people that inhabit it. I like to pretend I am an innocent when I approach these midway rip-offs, if only to hear the barkers give their speeches. If I am lucky, I take a photograph to capture the spirit of the event."

Amanda Wray uses storytelling as a means for everyday social activism. Disrupting, unsettling, and complicating as she goes. Amanda holds a PhD in rhetoric and composition from the University of Arizona, and she teaches as an assistant professor at the University of North Carolina at Asheville. She is a first-generation college student who learned the value of curiosity from her grandmother. Question everything.

⇒ MASTHEAD BIOGRAPHIES

Hunter Liguore, a multi-Pushcart Prize nominee, earned a BA in History and MFA in Creative Writing from Lesley University. Her stories have appeared in *Bellevue Literary Review, New Plains Review, The Irish Pages, Empirical Magazine, The Writer's Chronicle, DESCANT, Mason Road, The MacGuffin, Strange Horizons, Barely South Review, Rio Grande Review, Draft Journal, Amazing Stories,* and many more. In May 2013, her Calvino-style short story, "The Writer Who Slept for One Hundred Years," was inducted into the New Voices category by *The Master's Review*. She is the editor-in-chief of *American Athenaeum*. She revels in old legends, swords, and heroes. www.skytalewriter.com

John Dudek is an MFA candidate at Ohio State University and an English graduate of the University of Hartford. He is the poetry editor at *American Athenaeum*. He was named one of Connecticut's student poets in 2010 and his work has appeared in the *Connecticut Review, Writer's Block,* and elsewhere. His primary interests are urban decay, the role of the Lyric in contemporary thought, and the rusted fenders on classic motorcycles.

Jan M. G. Nerenberg holds a BA in Art, Creative Writing, and Literature from Pacific U in Forest Grove, Oregon, and an MFA in Creative Writing at Lesley University, and is currently pursuing a PhD in English/Creative Writing at Aberystwyth University in Wales. A Jack Kent Cook Scholar, she has been published in poetry, fiction and nonfiction. She's currently working on a young adult crossover novel, *Standing Stone*. Please visit her blog, "Right, Write, and Word-Wright." justjannerenberg.blogspot.com

Heidi C. Parton received her bachelor's degree in English literature from Augusta State University (now Georgia Regents University) and her MFA in creative writing from Lesley University. She primarily writes fiction and poetry and freelances as an editor. Heidi's poetry has been featured in *Sugar Mule, Obsession Lit Mag,* and *The Whirlwind Review*. She currently lives in South Carolina, with her husband, two cats, and dachshund mix. Interested parties can visit her website: heidicparton.com.

"Eden"

Photo taken by Chelsi and Chino Ruiz of Blackstar Photography

www.facebook.com/pages/Blackstar-Photography

DISCOVER NEW BOOKS

EXPLORE.

READ.

SAVOR.

DO SOMETHING NEW TODAY,
DISCOVER A NEW BOOK OR AUTHOR FROM
OUR
<u>DISCOVER NEW BOOKS</u>
SECTION

Things They Carry 176

"Peterson succeeds in demystifying the world of psychiatric care and challenging the stigma that continues to surround mental health."—*Kirkus Reviews*

LEAVE OF ABSENCE
TANYA J. PETERSON

Leave of Absence **by Tanya J. Peterson**

"Oliver knew deep in his heart that he would never, ever be better."

Leave of Absence is a story of loss and a story of strength. Oliver Graham is utterly bereft and laden with guilt in the aftermath of the traumatic deaths of his wife and son. He struggles with post-traumatic stress disorder, depression, and complicated mourning. Penelope Baker wrestles with schizophrenia and the devastating impact it has had on her once happy and successful life. Believing she is no longer loveable, she thinks the only thing she has left to give to her fiancée William is his freedom. Oliver and Penelope form a deep friendship that might be the key to their recovery. Readers join them on their tumultuous journey through pain, struggle, and triumphs. **Available at Amazon.com**

ABOUT SWORD & SAGA PRESS

At Sword & Saga Press our commitment is to our readers. Besides sourcing works of fiction from across the globe, we offer a place to talk books. We think of our press as the coliseum, the open fire, the desert range, the place to connect you with fiction that resonates a sense of nostalgia for the old days, while at the same time offering a view of the future.

The Last Man Anthology
A Mary Shelley Tribute.
Featuring Ray Bradbury, Barry N. Malzberg, and C. J. Cherryh. The anthology showcases short stories and poems that build on the theme of finality—of being last. Find it at Amazon.com

American Athenaeum
Subscribe today.
Don't be left at the train station.
Get your ticket now to the museum of words. Available through Amazon.com or Sword & Saga Press.

1 Bookshelf
Exploring Life's Little Experiences One Bookshelf at a Time. Visit today to share your own favorite books.
1bookshelf.blogspot.com.

Visit our website today: www.SwordandSagaPress.com.
Twitter: @SwordSagaPress ★ Facebook: WarriorsWanted

Printed in Great Britain
by Amazon.co.uk, Ltd.,
Marston Gate.